HE'S MY BABY, NOW

HE'S MY BABY, NOW

A Novel by Jeannette Eyerly

J. B. Lippincott Company/Philadelphia and New York

The characters in this book are fictitious and any resemblance they may bear to any persons living or dead is purely coincidental.

U.S. Library of Congress Cataloging in Publication Data

Eyerly, Jeannette.
  He's my baby, now.

  SUMMARY: A sixteen-year-old unwed father plots ways to keep the baby.
  [1. Unmarried fathers—Fiction] I. Title.
PZ7.E97He   [Fic]   77-23189
ISBN-0-397-31744-1

For
Naomi Burton Stone
with love

BOOK ONE

Where did you come from, baby dear?
Out of the everywhere into the here.
—George MacDonald,
At the Back of the North Wind

1
ANNOUNCEMENT

"Char-*ulls!*"

The voice comes ding-donging up the stairs like a musical doorbell. Charles, the object of the inquiry, burrows more deeply into the covers, tries unsuccessfully to retract his feet under the sheet which has pulled out from under the foot of the bed, and waits for the voice to come again.

It does. Only this time the cadence has shifted to "*Char*-ulls," on a descending note. An admonition is added. "It's a quarter past seven and I'm not going to call you again."

And she won't, either, thinks Charles. Call him again, that is. But she *will* take the handle of the broom and pound on the kitchen ceiling, which is under the floor of his bedroom, and keep it up until she hears the shower start to run.

Without any hope of sleeping another minute, Charles Penrose Elderbury gets out of bed. A "shrimp" until he was almost fourteen, he has grown five and a half inches in the last three years and by stretching he

11

stands six feet tall. For all of his rapid growth, however, he is compactly built and his body is as hairless as a baby's.

In the bathroom, he studies his face in the mirror. He finds there are only the same rather moldy-looking patches of fuzz that were there the day before. He decides against shaving. After the first few times, shaving is not the unalloyed pleasure he thought it would be.

When he comes into the kitchen twenty minutes later, his mother says, "Well, at last," but she says it without rancor and hands him a large glass of orange juice. While he drinks it, she puts a stack of pancakes, three sausage patties, a glass of milk, and a cup of coffee on the kitchen table before him. It is his favorite breakfast. He rewards her with a smile, but as her gaze is directed at his feet rather than his face, she misses it.

"Those sneakers," she says tersely, "are a disgrace. All that's holding them together are those filthy shoestrings. As soon as you finish your breakfast, you go right upstairs and put on your other ones."

"These *are* my other ones." He manages to sound both plaintive and defensive.

"They can't be. I haven't paid for them yet. I haven't even had the bill."

Charles, who should have paid for the shoes himself, extends a foot and gives the tattered bundle that encases it a critical look. "The uppers aren't in such good condition, but there's a lot of wear left in

12

the soles. Besides, at school everybody's sneakers look like this."

"I find that hard to believe," says his mother. She hesitates, knowing that she is going to say something she shouldn't, but the temptation is too great. "I dare say Dalton Smythe's sneakers don't look like that."

"Dalton Smythe!" The name drips from his lips with scorn. Dalton Smythe has been his cross, his albatross, his nemesis since they started kindergarten together. He says, "Dalton Smythe squats when he pees."

"Charles, I won't stand for that kind of talk and you know it."

He knows it. He gets around her when he can, but he does not relish a head-on confrontation. Through a mouthful of sausage and pancakes, Charles mumbles that he is sorry, though of course he is not. He wonders what his mother would think if she could hear the way the kids talk at school. If she heard the language that even some of the girls used, she'd think "squat when he pees" sounded genteel. And his mother is a lady. She can't help it. That's just the way she is.

She is also organized and he admires her for that.

Take this morning for example. Even though she is still messing around the kitchen fixing his breakfast, she's got her makeup on. Her long, sand-colored hair is neatly combed into a big, fat, pretzel-shaped thing she calls a chignon and underneath the striped apron, which almost covers her completely, he knows that she is dressed and ready to go to work as a private secretary to Mr. Morris Bascomb of the law firm of Bascomb, Teetlebaum, Parkerhouse, and Rogers. Not only that, but on a usual morning such as this is, she will have already cleaned up the house, put something in the Crock Pot for their dinner, and read the morning paper almost cover to cover. It is her custom, also, to "digest" the news for him while he eats his breakfast.

This she does now, sitting down at the table across from him with a cup of coffee and *The Cedar City Times-Herald* open before her.

"Eleven Moslems executed in Beirut," she says, "and they've kidnapped eleven more." She adds, as a sidebar, that she thinks both sides are to blame and that, what with the trouble in Northern Ireland and all, she doesn't know what the world is coming to.

She relays the news that the City Council has voted three to two to seal off the south entrance to Merrill Park. They hope that, by putting up a roadblock there, kids will be stopped from drag racing through the park at all hours of the day and night. She does not approve of the Council's action and prophesies that the first thing they know somebody will have rammed into the roadblock and gotten killed.

As she continues reading, Charles grunts, shakes his head, or intersperses a comment if the need arises. Charles rather likes his mother, though it is not advisable to say so publicly, and he appreciates her giving him the highlights of the news before he goes to school.

With his job at Farley's supermarket, where he works after school two days a week and half-days on Saturday, he sometimes doesn't have a chance to read the paper at all.

Pamela Elderbury is still going on. The Beatles are coming back together—or, at least, so it is rumored. The British pound has risen, New York City teachers are negotiating for higher wages, earth tremors have been felt in Nicaragua.

She glances up at the wall clock. Having promised Mr. Bascomb that she will come in early and work on some briefs that he will need in court that morning, she sees that it is time for her to go. She takes off her striped apron. Under it, she is wearing a dark gray flannel dress with white collar and cuffs. She reminds Charles to put his dishes in the sink when he is through eating and run water over them. And please, she says, don't forget your glasses. She leans over her son and brushes a kiss across the top of his head. There is scarcely a shade of difference between his hair and her own. Both also have the same wide-set dark blue eyes with long, curling lashes. It is in the lower half of Charles's face that a different set of genes is evident. His jaw is angular and he has a cleft in his chin.

"You *will* remember your glasses," his mother says again. "With what they cost, you can't afford to leave them sitting on your bureau."

Charles makes a noise that can be interpreted as a promise to remember. When his mother goes to the front closet and starts putting on her coat, he follows her. "How about me having the car? I've got time to drive you to work."

Pamela Elderbury shakes her head. "Not today, dear. I need it at noon to do an errand for Mr. Bascomb."

Charles is not expecting his mother to let him have the car and therefore is not disappointed. He does, however, experience a definite uneasiness at the second mention that morning of Mr. Bascomb who, since his wife's death several months before, seems to be occupying more and more of his mother's time and attention. (Now and then, for as long as he was old enough to know what she was doing, she has gone out with men friends but he never felt threatened by any of them as he does by this fellow Bascomb.)

Pamela Elderbury puts on a soft, knitted hat—for mid-April, the weather is still cold—glances at herself in the hall mirror, and then, with Charles paddling along behind her like a three-year-old, returns to the kitchen, where she pauses with one hand on the door leading to the attached garage.

"Oh, yes," she says. "There was something else in the paper I meant to ask you about. Didn't you, way last summer, go for a little while with a girl by the name of Daisy Dallinger?"

Charles said he did.

"I thought I remembered that name," says his mother. "And all I can say is that you're well rid of *her*. In fact, you're not going to believe it, but she's had a baby. There it was in the paper this morning, in the

16

births column, just as brazen as you please. *Ms.* Daisy Dallinger. Just like that." Her nose whitens a bit at the tip as she says, "*Ms.* Daisy Dallinger, *indeed.*" Then she goes out the door.

Before his mother has driven the car out of the garage, Charles begins fumbling through the pages of the newspaper which is still spread out on the kitchen table. He does not know where to look for the births column and some time passes before he finds it under the heading DAY'S RECORD. His heart is beating very fast as he runs his finger down the list. The names of the new parents are not given alphabetically and Daisy's name is almost at the bottom. The entry does not begin, as do all the others, with Mr. and Mrs., but says simply Ms. Daisy Dallinger, 1625 S.W. Fifth Street, a son, at the Hospital of the Immaculate Conception.

The word "son" rises up from the page and he feels as if his body is on fire. (It does not register on him that the address given is not where Daisy lives.) A second later he is shivering. "No way," he says to himself. "No way."

2
SCHOOL

Charles is late for school. This means that he has to go to the office to get a pink slip that will admit him to class, homeroom period now being over. He gives as his excuse that the alarm clock didn't go off. This is standard, and is accepted without so much as the raising of an eyebrow by Miss Grace Starbuck, who handles such things.

But he is still not in the clear.

The first class of the day is Junior English, taught by Mr. Herschel Baumgardner. Mr. Baumgardner, who looks like Ichabod Crane, fancies that he is a wit. When Charles comes in the door of Room 118, all eyes turn and Mr. Baumgardner says, "Ah, Charles! I was afraid that we were not going to have the pleasure of your company for the ides."

There is a titter of appreciation from the row of sycophants, Dalton Smythe among them, who sit directly in front of Mr. Baumgardner. Elsewhere in the classroom there is silence. Lucy Twining, who sits across the aisle from Charles, comments almost inaudi-

18

bly on Mr. Baumgardner's behavior in language that would put his mother into a state of shock.

Fortunately, Mr. Baumgardner does not hear what Lucy Twining says and continues in the same gross vein.

"Speaking of the ides," he says archly. "Charles, can you tell us about the ides? They did figure, you know, in our discussion of *Julius Caesar* last semester."

Charles, who has not yet pulled himself together, says he cannot remember anything about the ides.

Dalton Smythe, it turns out, can tell him. They are, says Dalton, an integral part of the old Roman calendar. There were the *calends,* the *nones,* and the *ides.* The calends fell on the first day of the month, the nones nine days before the ides, and the ides on the fifteenth. He goes on to tell more about the ides than anyone, including Mr. Baumgardner, wants to know. He says that the line "Beware the ides of March" occurs in Act I, Scene 2, and was spoken (he believes) by the Soothsayer. He adds that he could check it out, but even Mr. Baumgardner has had enough and turns the discussion toward *The Scarlet Letter,* which the class is reading—he fervently hopes not for the first time in their lives—along with *Rosemary's Baby.*

Mr. Baumgardner asks Charles if he can make a comparison between the two. Although Charles has read both books, he says he cannot. He is trying to remember the exact date that he and Daisy Dallinger did it for the last time. It was the day they agreed not

19

to see each other anymore but, because of all the conversation going on about Hester Prynne and the change in attitudes toward adultery since Hawthorne wrote *The Scarlet Letter,* he finds it impossible to determine whether the son born the day before to Ms. Daisy Dallinger could possibly be his.

3
SLEEPING

It could be.

He is late getting home, having worked at Farley's supermarket until eight o'clock, and does not have time to reach this conclusion until after dinner—which his mother had saved for him in the Crock Pot—when he is up in his room pretending to study.

The only possibility that the baby is *not* his is if Daisy was sleeping with someone else at the same time she was sleeping with him. (For several reasons, he does not think this is likely.) He wonders why making love is called "sleeping together." He and Daisy never slept as much as a minute. About the only time they ever even closed their eyes was when they kissed and they did not always close them then. He liked looking, close up, into Daisy's eyes and she, she said, liked looking into his.

Daisy's eyes, as he remembers them, are emerald green surrounded by a broad ring of mossy brown with darker brown tadpoles swimming around in them. (She says they are called "hazel.") The pupils are enormous, jet black, liquid, and shiny.

There is no doubt that "sleeping" is the wrong word. What they did was to thrash around and laugh a lot.

He remembers that once when they were right in the middle of doing it they fell off the raft into the middle of Lake Larkspur. The lake was once a gravel pit, and the spot where they fell off is about eighty feet deep, though some say it is bottomless. But even the mention of the word "bottomless," which Charles just happened to mention, struck them as funny and they swam around in the icy cold water—Daisy swimming like a fish—until they were out of breath and then they climbed onto the raft and lay side by side looking up at the stars.

Pamela Elderbury comes upstairs and says she is going to bed. She thinks it would be a good idea if Charles went to bed too as tomorrow is a school day. For Chrissakes, he thinks. As if he didn't know tomorrow is a school day. He says he will go to bed as soon as he finishes studying. He does, in fact, open his trig book and write down the first of the problems. But he makes no attempt to work it. Instead, he thinks some more about Daisy and how it all began.

4
THE RAFT

It is the last week of May and the day of the sophomore class picnic at Lake Larkspur. The several hundred kids from Cedar City High School, however, are not the only ones there. Three large yellow buses with MIDDLE VALLEY SCHOOL DISTRICT painted on their sides in black letters are already in the parking lot when the Cedar City sophomores arrive. So there are kids playing softball, eating, necking, or just plain horsing around, all over the place.

Although it's still a little cold for swimming, about mid-afternoon he decides to go for a swim anyway and is glad he's brought his bathing trunks. He is about halfway out to the raft, which is anchored a good quarter of a mile from shore, before he sees that someone is lying on it. Charles is a good swimmer—though not quite good enough to make the CCHS swimming team—and in another minute or two he sees the "someone" is a girl. She is wearing a black bikini and it consists of little more than some scraps of material above and below, held together by a few knots and strings, as needed. She is lying face down, her head away from him. There's so little of her—she's really tiny—that, in her black suit with nothing but suntanned skin in between, she is almost invisible on the wooden planks which have been fastened somehow to a bunch of empty oil drums.

Even so, with eyes that are daily growing more nearsighted, he sees that her smallness is not a handicap. Everything is very properly arranged, though on a small scale. Her long black hair lies spread out on her bare back like seaweed.

He hoists himself, arms straight, muscles extending, halfway out of the water. (He still works out occasionally with barbells.) He is only sorry that, because she is facing away from him, she cannot see how gracefully (he thinks) he clambers aboard the raft.

He says, "Hullo"—surely a safe enough salutation—but there the script, as he is writing it, goes awry.

Without turning her head, without even a twitch of a muscle, she says, "Would you kindly get the hell off this raft or I'll scream."

Her tone is so venomous that he immediately rolls off the raft into the water without even thinking that he has as much right to be there as she has. He swims round the raft hoping to see her face, but all that is visible is one brown sea-green eye considering him from behind a veil of hair.

"Oh, shit," she says at last, grudgingly. "Get back on, if you want to. I was afraid you were someone else."

Charles once again clambers aboard the raft but

keeps at a discreet distance, the way one does with a dog that has snarled one warning but, after that, may bite. She rolls over on her back and lies with her arms in a kind of cradle beneath her head. This pushes her breasts almost over the top half of the bikini. They are not brown like the rest of her that he can see, but as white and round as dumplings or untoasted bagels. He stares at them until he is embarrassed, but she does not even seem aware of his presence. When he looks at her face, he sees that tears are leaking out of her eyes and running unevenly down her cheeks. "It's not you," the girl says finally. "Just don't talk, I've had enough talking to last me a lifetime."

Charles says he won't talk, and he doesn't. He just lies there, feeling happy and vaguely excited. The sun warms his body without cooking it, and a breeze blows across the surface of the lake so that the raft rocks as gently as if he were lying on a water bed. He thinks he would like to own a water bed. His friend Jeff Kline has one. Perhaps, after he has enough money saved to buy a car—since he got his regular job at Farley's supermarket his bank account is really growing—he will buy a water bed. It will have to go in the basement though. That's where Jeff Kline's is. His mother would never allow it upstairs for fear it would spring a leak and flood the whole house.

He feels his eyelids fluttering as somnolence creeps over him. A rather sharp jab in the solar plexus suddenly brings him to life. The girl is leaning over, her hair swinging, her breasts popping, looking down at him.

"Hey," she says, "have you got a father?"

Charles says, "What?" although he has heard.

"Are you deaf or something?" the girl says. "I asked you a simple, ordinary question. Have you got a father?"

Charles still hesitates. The subject of his father is a delicate one and he does not like the idea of a total stranger, even if she has these amazing eyes that look like a dark lake in the middle of a forest, asking questions about him.

The girl seems to sense this. At least, she doesn't sound truculent when she sits back on her heels and says she didn't mean anything. She was just asking.

This takes the sting out of the question and Charles, who doesn't mind anyone knowing that his parents are divorced—at least half of the kids in his class have parents who aren't living together—finally tells her he has a father. Someplace. At least, as far as he knows he has one. He hasn't been around lately.

The truth of it is that his father has not been around for as long as he can remember. This absence, however, has not prevented Charles (not only secretly, but publicly) from fantasizing about him a lot. The fantasizing results in a father far more splendid than any of his friends' flesh and blood fathers. Though he admits that Jeff Kline's father is good, really good: He does all the things a kid's father ought to do—at least when the kid is young—like taking him fishing, going to ball games, camping out overnight, and things like that.

Although for a long time now Charles hasn't told anyone that his father is a mining engineer in Central America, or that his father gave him the ten-speed bike that was really given to him by his Grandmother Penrose, he still would not be too surprised if his father did turn up someday. Just out of the blue. And with an awfully good excuse for being out of touch all these years.

The girl reaches over the edge of the raft and skims a leaf from the water. It is an oak leaf. Charles wonders how it got out there in the middle of the lake. If a bird was carrying it, or what.

When she starts tearing the leaf apart, first down the middle, then along the various veins and segments, Charles notices that she bites her fingernails. There is a little plump pincushion of flesh at the end of every finger.

"I wish mine wasn't," says the girl.

"You wish yours wasn't what?" asks Charles, who has lost the thread of what scarcely could be called a conversation.

"I wish *my* father wasn't around."

"Why's that?" asks Charles cautiously. "What did he do?"

"*Do?*" The girl spits out the word, for she is angry again. "What *doesn't* he do?" Her color rises

26

and her soft mouth trembles. "You'd think I was a . . . a whore or something. I can't go anyplace, do anything, that he isn't spying on me. When I heard somebody climbing on the raft, I thought maybe it was him."

"Doesn't he work?"

"Work? *Him?* You've got to be kidding." She laughs, not a real laugh, but enough of one to make two dimples he didn't know she had appear. "I work, my mom works, my Aunt Nelda works, even my eleven-year-old sister Indigo has part of a paper route. But not my father. Oh, no."

He says that is too bad, but the remark is a mistake, for she immediately retorts that whether her father works or not is no concern of his.

Charles would like to say that she was the one who brought the subject up, but he is afraid it would make her even madder. He reflects that he has never met anyone who can blow hot and cold so fast. For now she is contrite and saying she's sorry, and that it's not his fault, and that she doesn't know what makes her such a bitch except that it's about time for her to fall off the roof.

Charles knows what she is talking about, although he has never heard it called "falling off the roof." Even so, he thinks it sounds better than the expression "on the rag." He knows, of course, that it's called other things too. He remembers how, when he was younger, he'd wondered quite a bit what went on during a girl's period. Like how much blood she lost.

27

And why it was that girls didn't want you to know when their period was.

Sometime during the last year in junior high a couple of sex counselors had come to school and talked to the girls and then to the boys. They'd cleared up a lot of questions Charles had had then, but one worry had persisted—exactly what do you do when you have intercourse and would he know what to do when the time came. This he was able to find out himself—with Daisy.

That is the reason he is sitting there with a hard-on when his mother knocks at his door. She wants to know if he is still studying. When he says "yes," she adds that it is one o'clock in the morning and that she wants that light out right now. Just as if he were in kindergarten instead of about to finish tenth grade and only two months away from seventeen.

Suddenly, however, he is very tired. Less than five minutes later he is undressed, in bed, and asleep. The next morning his pajamas are a mess.

5
NO SHOW

Charles works at Farley's supermarket from four to eight o'clock in the afternoon on Tuesdays and Thursdays and on Saturdays from eight A.M. until noon.

Usually, he sacks. Standing beside the checker, he puts the groceries in a big double sack after the checker has run them through. Sometimes, however, he works in the "shed," an addition at one side of the big rambling building. Here, shoppers drive their cars in to pick up the sacks of groceries that are too heavy or too numerous for them to carry. Shoppers hold up a plastic tag with a number on it that they have been given, and the carhop carries their groceries from the cart with the corresponding number to the customer's automobile.

Charles likes his job and feels fortunate to have it. He particularly likes it when he is assigned to carhopping. Whatever the weather, it is refreshing to get out of the supermarket with its approximately one hundred thousand smells into the fresh air. He is warm-blooded. Even when it's down below zero, like the winter just past, he never puts on a jacket. He likes getting the icy air. He likes hearing the customers say, "Aren't you freezing?" Or, "You'll catch your death of pneumonia, dear." It is always women who talk like this, and Charles likes women. However, he likes men who say, "The cold doesn't bother you a bit, does it, son?" Usually this is the kind of man who very likely isn't wearing a hat himself and isn't muffled to his ears in a car coat.

Moreover, the pay at Farley's supermarket is good. Since he turned sixteen last June, now almost a year ago, he makes, as do the other part-time help, three dollars an hour plus a discount on anything purchased from the store. Since he was ten years old, Charles has always had a job of some kind—pulling weeds, mowing lawns, shoveling snow, carrying a paper route, even occasionally baby-sitting—but until he went to work at Farley's, his income was a pretty chancy thing. That is why, last August thirtieth, it had hurt him so much to draw out one hundred and fifty bucks from what he thinks of as the savings of a lifetime to give to Daisy for the abortion.

There is no doubt about the date he gave her the money because he found the withdrawal slip— after a good deal of searching—where he had hidden it with a whole bunch of other stuff, in a bureau drawer. (As far as his mother knows that money is still earning four and three-fourths percent interest at the Cedar City National Bank.)

Waiting for the bus—one of two he will need to take to get him to the Hospital of the Immaculate Conception—he reflects about this. If he still had the money he gave Daisy, he'd now have almost enough to buy the Heap of the Week, which is sitting in Dave Pinkerton's used car lot on the corner of Tenth and Telford.

On the bus, he goes past Farley's supermarket. It is Wednesday and Bob Borg, a kid he knows, is working the four to eight o'clock shift. Charles sees Bob outside the shed piling groceries into somebody's Caddie. A dozen blocks farther on, the bus passes Pinkerton's used car lot, but the Heap of the Week is gone. Somebody's grabbed it. Charles thinks Dave Pinkerton's idea is a good one. In essence, Pinkerton is saying, "This car I'm advertising is not the greatest thing on wheels. In fact, it's something of a heap. It needs new tires, new shocks, and a paint job—or whatever—but for anybody who wants to go to the trouble of fixing it up, this Ford LTD is worth every cent and more of the nine hundred and ninety-nine dollars and ninety-nine cents I'm asking for it."

Charles is sorry that the LTD is gone, but he knows that next week Dave Pinkerton will have another one out there on display that's maybe an even better buy.

At Sixth and Grove Street in downtown Cedar City, Charles gets off the bus and waits a good twenty minutes before a Number Fourteen bus comes along.

Number Fourteen will take him within a block of the Hospital of the Immaculate Conception, where Ms. Daisy Dallinger is "confined."

Confined! Charles thinks. What a word. It sounds more like a patient in a lunatic asylum.

He is, in fact, a little nervous about going to the hospital at all. He has not been inside one since he was three years old and had his tonsils and adenoids out. He does not know whether he remembers the experience or whether it is one of the stories that he has heard his mother repeat so many times that he *thinks* he remembers. As long as she does not tell it in front of anyone, he rather enjoys hearing how, when his mother was allowed in to see him after the surgery, he stood up in his little crib and said, "This is the saddest day of my life."

The Hospital of the Immaculate Conception is huge although it did not start out that way. The original structure, built in the early nineteen hundreds, had been torn down wing by wing as new units were added.

At first, Charles cannot find the door to go in; then, once inside the building, it is like being set loose in a labyrinth. True, there is a white-haired woman, in a smock the color of canned salmon, sitting at a desk with an INFORMATION sign on it, who directs him to the maternity floor by means of an elevator and a complicated set of instructions.

He gets to the fourth floor, but then has to stop two different people and ask them where to go. These directions lead him down corridors as long as a city block. These corridors are carpeted in pale green and, except for a faintly antiseptic smell, resemble those of a first-class motel. Two summers ago, when Charles and his mother drove to Cincinnati to spend a week with his Aunt Elaine, they stayed in such a place.

At his third stop for information, he finds that he is already there. He is in the maternity ward and doesn't know it. He asks embarrassedly if he can see the babies, but is told by a grim-faced woman with several morbid black stripes on her cap that he is too late for the "showing." (It is, he thinks, more like a movie theater than a hospital. "Sorry, sir, but the feature has already started. No one else will be seated until the next showing." There's probably even a sign out front advising that the show is rated R or PG only.)

He asks Black Stripes when that will be and is told that the afternoon showing is just over and that there won't be another one until seven o'clock that night.

Charles is enfolded in such gloom that the nurse with the black stripes asks whose baby it is that he wanted to see.

The word "mine" springs to Charles's lips, but he stifles it. There will be no baby in the nursery named Elderbury. He forces himself to mutter, "The Dallinger baby."

"Oh," says the nurse. *"Oh!"* And she gives Charles a look that would wilt lettuce.

6
CHINS

Charles does not know how he'll manage to get back to the hospital by seven o'clock that night for the showing. However, when he gets home, his mother tells him with rather restrained excitement that she is going out to dinner with Mr. Bascomb. Although this new relationship between his mother and her boss continues to make him uneasy, in this instance it gives him leverage in asking her if he can have the car to go over to Jeff Kline's house to study.

Pamela Elderbury considers overlong, then says she guesses Charles can have the car. But he must not be late and he must be careful.

Before Charles can express his thanks, he remembers that he has hemmed himself in. Unless he gets to the hospital before eight o'clock he will miss the second showing.

This means he must tell another lie. So he says he must leave early enough to go to the main library downtown and pick up an absolutely essential book for American Government *before* going to Jeff's house.

By this time, however, Pamela Elderbury's mind is on what she will wear to go out with Mr. Bascomb, and after ritualistically extracting a promise from Charles that he will eat a good dinner, be careful, and come home early, she guesses that will be all right and goes upstairs to get ready.

Charles eats a good dinner—he seldom has been known not to—and he is ready to leave by a quarter of seven. This is good timing, for Mr. Bascomb is not due to pick up his mother until seven thirty, and if he never meets Mr. Bascomb this will be too soon.

Even though they charge for parking, the hospital parking lot is crowded when he gets there and he drives around for ten minutes before he finds a place to put his mother's Toyota. By the time he reaches the maternity floor, a dozen or more people are already crowding around a long window behind which, he presumes, they keep the babies.

He finds the showing is just about to start and hangs back, waiting to see how they go about it.

The process does not seem to be complicated. Someone gives the name of the baby they want to see to a woman wearing a mask and muffled in white, who is inside the nursery. She walks up and down the aisles and reaches down into a row of boxlike cribs, scoops up a bundle scarcely recognizable as a baby, and holds it close to the window for all to see.

As she does this, an elderly woman wearing a large lavender orchid says, "Oooooh! *Look* at him! Isn't he gorgeous?"

35

Then everybody standing around says, "Oooooh! Look at him!" though it is obvious that not everybody agrees with the description of "gorgeous." Charles edges closer. As far as he can see, the swaddled infant on view looks like a piece of raw meat with a few rudimentary features. It is crying.

The woman with the orchid dabs at her eyes with a handkerchief and steps back. It has been too much for her. Meanwhile, that baby is put away and another one brought forward for inspection.

Charles scrutinizes each one as it is presented.

Although to him the babies are almost identical —all are wrinkled, red as beets, and have foreheads that sort of fold down over their eyes—the babies' friends and relatives seem to find startling resemblances either to themselves or other members of the family. One observer says, "Oh, Tom! She has your eyes!" Another baby, it is said, has Gloria's hairline. And still another has inherited Grandfather Allen's nose. Charles pities them all.

Soon, he is the only one left in front of the viewing window, all the others having disappeared into hospital rooms where the babies' mothers are holding court.

As Charles continues to hang around, the woman in the nursery gives him an inquiring look.

He says, "Dallinger," but his mouth is so dry he is not certain that she hears him so he says it again, this time so loudly that it frightens him.

The woman goes away and when she comes back her eyes behind the mask are smiling.

This baby is sleeping.

This baby is neither red nor wrinkled.

This baby is pink.

His hair is brushed up into a little peak on top of a head that doesn't look as if someone had given it a good smack just after he was born.

This baby is smiling. It is a little one-sided smile that comes and goes, then comes again.

But this is not all. There is an unmistakable cleft in the tiny chin. He turns away from the window because he does not want the woman to see that there are tears in his eyes.

7
MONEY

Charles does not understand his emotions. He only knows that until the very moment he saw the baby he has believed that there might be some mistake, a possibility that the baby is not his. Perhaps Daisy *was* sleeping with someone else while she was sleeping with him.

But now all the theory and speculation about the baby being his is out the window. The chin proves it. He lays a forefinger in the cleft of his own chin and pushes the flesh up on either side of it. Until that moment he has hated his chin, though girls profess to love it. It is the only part of his body, up to now, he has really hated.

He feels a stirring in his chest unlike any that he has ever before experienced. *His* baby is obviously superior to any of the dozen or more babies shown previously that evening. (His baby is probably superior to *all* the other babies in the nursery.) Anybody with eyes in his head, he tells himself, could see that his baby is bigger. Also heavier. The nurse had used both arms to carry him. All the others she had cradled along the length of one arm.

His baby is, well . . . incredible.

Charles feels an overwhelming desire to tell someone about this baby and its superiority. But there is no one he dares talk to except Daisy. He has not seen her for more than seven months—last August thirtieth, which was the date he drew the one hundred and fifty dollars out of his savings account and gave it to Daisy for the abortion.

It had about killed him to give it to her, but at that time it seemed better—*anything* would have seemed better—than getting married.

Standing outside Daisy's hospital room trying to get up enough nerve to go in, Charles remembers the day late last summer when she called him on the phone. At that time, almost a month had passed since they had broken up and he was not at all pleased to hear from her. After all, breaking up was as much her idea as his, both of them agreeing that they liked each other as much as ever but that everything had just gotten too complicated. Just too damned difficult. Everything always on the sly. Daisy's father watching her like a hawk. Both of them having to tell so many lies you couldn't keep track of them. And always the Lake Larkspur Park police, those sadistic bastards, going around the park with their big flashlights trying to catch you with your pants down. Once, one of them had taken off his uniform and swum out to the raft hoping to catch them. And if it wasn't for Daisy being able to hold her breath underwater for as long as he could, they would have been caught for sure.

But anyway, just before school was about to start, there was Daisy on the phone saying, "Elderbury, meet me tomorrow afternoon at Lake Larkspur. There by the picnic tables."

Daisy does not say, "Will you?" or, "Can you?" but just plain, "Meet me."

He doesn't want to meet her, but he does—there had been this kind of funny note in Daisy's voice —and there she is, sitting on one of the picnic tables with about ten thousand sets of initials carved in it, swinging her legs. They are bare and brown, her sandaled feet dusty from the long walk from the bus line. Her skirt barely covers the bulge of her small, neat bottom.

She tosses her long dark hair back from her face and says, "Sorry, Elderbury, but we've got to get married." Just like that.

He hates it when she calls him "Elderbury," almost as much as he hates it when she talks gutter talk, though he's reasonably sure she does it just to irritate him. He braces himself. "Married," he says faintly. "Why?"

"Shit," says Daisy. "Why do you suppose? Because I'm pregnant. That's why."

He does not say anything because he can't. He is struck dumb.

Presently, Daisy puts one of her small brown hands, with fingernails still bitten down to the quick, on one of his—with which he is hanging on to the picnic table so he won't fall down—and says, "We can get a divorce right afterward. I don't want to get married any more than you do."

Then she adds that if they don't get married her father will kill her.

Having heard many stories during the almost two months they went together about her terrible-tempered father, he believes her father *might* kill her.

"How . . ." he says, his voice cracking, "how about an abortion?"

She shakes her head and says she doesn't think she could do that.

Time passes. An oak leaf sails down, this way and that, on a little current of air. She picks it up and begins to dismember it as she did that day on the raft.

He is not touched. It all seems to be Daisy's fault for not taking proper precautions. Besides, she is the one who started it by taking off her bathing suit. Finally he says, "I'm sorry, Daisy, but I'm not getting married and that is that."

She begins to cry. But it is not noisy crying. The tears just leak out of those mossy, emerald green eyes and dribble like a leaky faucet down her cheeks. "O.K.," she says, with a little whimper. "I'd get an abortion if I had any money."

"*I've* got money," he says, just like he was one of the Rockefellers. "How much would it take? I mean, about?"

Daisy sniffs and wipes her eyes with the back of her hands. "I know a girl who got one for a hundred and fifty dollars. It wouldn't be more than that."

Except for any interest that is accruing, Charles knows to the nickle how much money he has in his savings account. Before Daisy can change her mind, he hands her his handkerchief, which is reasonably clean, and says briskly, "Well, then, that's settled. We'll get the money right away."

Daisy goes with him to the bank, but stands back well away from the teller's window while he gets the money.

The teller asks him how he wants it and Charles has to think for a minute before he realizes that the man is asking in what denominations he wants the money.

"A century," says Charles. He has heard Jeff

Kline's father talking about century notes and he likes the sound of it. "And a fifty."

The teller shoves the withdrawal receipt and the two bills through the window and Charles picks them up. He has never had this much money in his possession before—in fact, he's never even seen a hundred dollar bill—and although he wonders briefly if there might not be some other way out than giving it to Daisy, he knows there is none.

"Thanks, Elderbury," Daisy says. She doesn't even look at the money, which she stuffs in a coin purse, then into the ratty-looking shoulder bag which she always carries. It is made of burlap and has a lot of strings hanging down.

Charles offers to drive Daisy home—having Jeff Kline's car at his disposal has made everything a little easier—but she refuses. He then says, "Well, good-bye, Daisy. And good luck." He hears the words coming out of his body, but they sound as if they were spoken by a robot. And the funny thing is that he's not really seeing Daisy. Her face is swimming around. He tells her he has something in his eye. Daisy has something in her eye, too. They shake hands.

That was the way it ended.

After about a week he didn't even think about her anymore. Not too often anyway. But now all that is changed.

The door to Daisy's hospital room is slightly ajar. Taking a deep breath, he walks in.

8
REUNION

Charles is not expecting a warm welcome, but he does not expect all hell to break loose.

He does not expect Daisy, with remarkably good aim, to throw a book at him, nor does he anticipate that when he stoops to pick it up—it is a paperback copy of *Silent Spring*—she will throw her plastic water pitcher at him and hit him in the head.

As the book, followed by the water pitcher, sails through the air, one of the other three new mothers in the room screams. Another falls back on her pillow in a simulated faint and the third yells, "Oh, nurse!" All the visitors rise up in alarm.

Almost immediately, a fierce voice from the doorway demands to know what is going on.

Charles picks himself up from the floor to face the nurse with the black stripes who had wilted him that afternoon.

"You," she says pejoratively—in a voice which reminds Charles of the sign at the zoo advising visitors not to feed the animals—then adds, "I might have

known I would find *you* in here disturbing the *mothers*."
She looks around, surveying the damage, then says
coldly, "I am afraid that I shall have to ask you to leave."

Charles is willing to leave, but before he can
reach the door Daisy says, surprisingly, that he can stay
if he wants to. She tells the nurse that Charles didn't
do anything at all. She says that she was the one who
threw the book and the water pitcher.

The nurse's anger, however, is not assuaged, for
she now glares at Daisy, tells her that no further dis-
turbance will be tolerated, and then stalks out.

"Come here, Charles," says Daisy.

Charles slinks toward the bed and sits down in
the straight-backed chair that Daisy indicates.

"Draw the curtains."

"What curtains?"

"Those curtains, stupid." Daisy points to some
bunched-up, pea-green curtains that are hanging from
a track at the head of the bed. "Pull them around on
that metal thing."

Charles, who has not noticed either the curtains
or the metal thing, does as he is told and he and Daisy
are immediately enclosed in a small green room. It is a
little (but not much) like being under water.

From outside the curtain, there come several
gasps of disapproval and a good deal of noisy clucking
and whispering.

Daisy advises him not to pay any attention. She
says that the women in her room are all bitches. And
the nurse who (just now) told him he would have to

44

leave is the worst bitch of all. She then tells Charles that the green curtains are for privacy and that she has the right to close them if she wants to. "The nurses pull them around when they are going to do something to you," she adds. "And the doctors."

Charles wonders what kind of things they do to Daisy but he does not want to ask. In fact, until Daisy mentions it, he has been so busy thinking about the baby that he has not thought at all about Daisy's part in the affair.

In the pale green light Charles looks at Daisy, who is sitting up in bed. The lower half of her is covered with a rumpled sheet. On her upper half she is wearing some kind of a blue jacket thing (which doesn't suit her at all) with a lot of lace and ribbons on it. He notices that her tan is gone—after all, whose isn't?—but she looks all right. Except for her chest. Something has happened to her chest. It is huge. He cannot help but remember how it was before.

Daisy is in a conciliatory mood. "Did I hurt you when I threw the pitcher and book?" she asks sweetly.

Charles says "no," though his shoulder still hurts a little. He has to remind himself that Daisy is a switch-hitter. That she blows hot one minute and cold the next.

"I am sorry I threw those things at you," says Daisy contritely. "I only did it because I didn't want you to find out about the baby." Although this state-ment is completely irrational, she says it as if it explained everything. "How did you find out, anyway?" she asks.

He tells her it was in yesterday's paper. In the births column.

Daisy bites her lip so hard that small white marks show. She'd forgotten completely, she says, that births are printed in the paper. "I hope your mother doesn't know. That would be too bad."

"She's the one who told me," says Charles. "Fortunately, she didn't put two and two together."

"Or one and one." Daisy gives him a brilliant smile, then holds her hand over her mouth to stifle her laughter.

Charles laughs too, but it is not the same as when they laughed at Lake Larkspur and fell off the raft into the deep water. Now he has other things on his mind.

He would really like to know what is wrong with Daisy's chest—he can't keep his eyes away from it —and if it's permanent. (Not that it would make any difference to him, he tells himself, for now he feels nothing for Daisy at all, nothing at all.) He would also like to know what happened to the money he gave her for the abortion. Although he's glad she didn't have it —he is doing a good job of forgetting that he was the one who suggested it—he'd be interested in knowing the reason *why*.

The last two questions, however, are heavy ones and he doesn't know whether this is the time or the place to ask them. Instead, he points to her chest and, even then, phrases his question discreetly. "It . . . ah . . . seems a little bigger."

Daisy glances down at herself. "Oh, that," she says. She lays a hand on the shelf under the bed jacket that rises up almost under her chin. "That's milk. And an ice bag. Nothing to worry about. They're just trying to get rid of it."

Charles looks bewildered. "Get rid of the ice bag?"

"The milk, stupid," says Daisy. "They're drying it up." She has suddenly turned irascible. "You didn't think, did you, for God's sake, that just because I *had* this baby I was going to *nurse* it?"

Charles does not know how to reply. Although he sees lots of young babies and their mothers in the store, he has never seen a baby *nurse*. In any case, the thought of Daisy having *milk* in her, or of her nursing a baby, has never entered his mind.

"I guess not," he says at last.

Other people might have lost the thread of the conversation, but not Daisy. She is quick about everything. "I am glad of that," she says. "I am *very* glad of that. Now, are there any further questions?"

Questions! He has a hundred of them. But with Daisy as she is right now, he is afraid to ask them. He does decide, however, that it will be safe to talk about the baby. "He's super, isn't he?" says Charles. "The baby, I mean. I saw him just before I came in here. He's the biggest one they've got." Charles's voice becomes a little tremulous.

47

Daisy only looks at him.

"And he isn't red, either," Charles goes on. In his mind's eye, he is seeing the baby lying in the nurse's arms, the little smile coming and going on his lips. He is also seeing the little cleft in his chin. With great restraint he does not mention this, which is fortunate.

For Daisy, who has picked up her water glass and finds it empty—the pitcher she threw at Charles having been taken away to be sterilized and not yet returned—slams the glass down on the table. "If you say one more word about that baby, I am going to scream."

Although Daisy looks as if she means it—her fists are clenched and her mouth half open—Charles must ask the all-compelling question. "Why?"

Daisy explodes. Her voice trembles. "Why? Because *I* haven't seen him, that's why. Even if I *wanted* to see him, they wouldn't let me. It's a rule."

"A rule?" Charles repeats. "What kind of a rule is it that you can't see your own baby?" In his relief, he begins to laugh. It is all so ridiculous. A second later, Daisy is laughing, too. A curious laugh, for at the same time she seems to be crying. "Don't you know *anything?* I don't know how you can be so stupid and live. Don't you know you're not allowed to see your baby if you're giving him away?"

As they are talking, bells ring noisily in the corridor outside. Guests in the room are saying good-bye and leaving. But Charles does not hear them. He is sitting hunched in an attitude of bewilderment and despair when the pea-green curtain is jerked back and a nurse Charles has not seen before is standing there. She is carrying a tray of evil-looking little vials and unpleasant-looking equipment.

He does not move.

"Visiting hours are over," says this person coldly. "I think you'd better go."

"Yes," says Daisy, "and they are over *permanently.*" Her eyes are as cold as bullets. "So you might as well stop hanging around. I never want to see you again."

9
MAKING OUT

Although Charles does not remember driving home, he must have done so without incident, for a half hour later, a little after nine thirty, he turns into his own drive.

But he cannot drive the car into the garage, for another car is parked ahead of him. The beam of the Toyota's headlight first picks up the Cadillac insignia on the rear end. Then a shadowy figure on the front seat almost immediately turns into *two* figures.

49

Charles switches off the Toyota's headlights and sits there, not knowing what to do. It is too much that on the same evening he has learned that his only son is to be given away, he should find his mother making out with Mr. Bascomb.

10
THE FIRST TIME

Charles lets himself in with his own house key. His mother gave it to him on his twelfth birthday because by then he was presumed to be "responsible," which, in other words and among other things, meant not losing it. Before then—and after he was old enough not to have to have after-school arrangements made for him—the key was left in a secret hiding place so he could let himself into the house before his mother got home from work.

Tonight, before going out for the evening, Pamela Elderbury has left a light on in the living room. It is a pleasant, comfortable room with easy chairs and two long, extra-soft, cretonne-covered sofas that you are allowed to put your feet on. The sofas face each other in front of a fireplace that, in winter, burns a real fire a good deal of the time. There are books, magazines, stereo equipment, and a table-model television set in black and white. Except for several pots of healthy-looking ivy and a late-blooming amaryllis in full flower, nothing is sitting around doing nothing in this room. (Charles has a friend whose mother collects small china objects. It is impossible to move around in that house without knocking something off a table and breaking it.)

Charles walks into his own living room without seeing it.

Upstairs, he undresses in the dark and, feeling cheated and betrayed, he lies down on his bed with his arms cradled under his head. He does not understand the emotions that are coursing through him like a river that has suddenly found a new channel.

But if he does not understand himself or his emotions, he does not understand Daisy, either. Giving away a perfectly good baby! It is incomprehensible. But this baby is more than a "perfectly good baby"; he is superior. Charles wonders why Daisy had this baby if she did not intend to keep him.

Lying there, Charles does not find it at all incongruous that he should have these thoughts, though less than forty-eight hours ago he did not even know that he *had* a baby.

The luminous dial of the alarm clock on his bureau shows that it is ten minutes before eleven. He has been home an hour and twenty minutes and his mother has not yet come upstairs. He gets up and looks out of his bedroom window although he knows that he

51

cannot possibly see the driveway and Mr. Bascomb's car from that vantage point. He wishes his mother would come to bed. It does not seem proper that a woman of her age, and at that hour of the night, should be sitting in a parked car making out.

He lies back down on the bed but he does not go to sleep. Once more he is thinking about Daisy and the baby and when they might have made it.

He doesn't think it should be too hard to figure out. After the day they met on the raft—which doesn't really count because all they do then is talk—until early August when they break up, they only see each other four times.

The first real time is shortly after school is out. They arrange to meet at ten o'clock in the morning (if the weather is nice) at the entrance to the park. Although they both take the bus—Daisy clear from hell and gone from the other side of town and outside the city limits—they arrive within fifteen minutes of each other. They shed their clothes right away, each going behind a tree, then plunge into the icy water and start out to the raft.

About a dozen yards before they reach it, Daisy disappears.

Since they have left the shore, he is swimming ahead of her—though not too far ahead, because he does not wish to win by too large a margin—but every so often he looks over his shoulder to be sure she's coming along all right. And she always is. Once when he looks she is doing a very fast and efficient crawl.

Another time she is doing the breaststroke. When she comes up to breathe, she is blowing air like a porpoise. Most of her long dark hair is flowing behind her and the rest of it is as tightly fitted to her skull as if it were painted on.

But now when he looks there is no Daisy.

He is gripped by a terrible fear.

The surface of the lake is calm, almost opaque. He calls her name loudly and in the process gets a mouthful of water that almost drowns him. He turns back toward the shore for help, though he knows there will be no help when he gets there. At this hour of the morning, Lake Larkspur is as deserted as an atoll in the Pacific.

Then he hears someone call *his* name. It is Daisy. She is sitting on the edge of the raft swinging her legs and laughing. While he is floundering around, drowning, she has swum underwater and got to the raft before him.

Charles clambers on the raft. He is mad, really mad at Daisy for frightening him half to death but he can't stay that way. For Daisy hasn't a stitch on. Though, in a way, it looks as if she has her bikini on in reverse. Where the skimpy little halter top and diaperlike pants have covered her, she is white. She is nut-brown everywhere else.

It is the first time he has ever seen a girl stark naked and he doesn't know where to look.

Daisy tells him to take his trunks off. You would if you were a model, she says, primly. So he does. Not because of that argument about being a model, though, but because it would have seemed impolite not to.

Almost at once, he gets a hard-on and Daisy screams, giving him the distinct impression that this is the first time she has witnessed this fascinating and somehow alarming phenomenon. When he chases her, she dives off the raft. Not until quite a bit later do they start fooling around. At first, it doesn't come off too well, but finally he gets it in and gets the job done. Afterward he feels fine, but he's not so sure about Daisy. She just sits there on the raft, her knees hunched up to her chin, and nibbles at her fingernails though there's nothing there to bite. She says she hopes that now her father will be satisfied.

Charles hears the stairs creak and his mother go softly down the hall to her room. So that worry is off his mind. He turns over on his side and goes to sleep.

11
THE NEW LOOK

Charles Penrose Elderbury is one of the one thousand eight hundred and sixty-two kids enrolled in the senior high division of Cedar City High School. Like all schools everywhere, good kids, bad kids, and kids in between go there. (This makes it easy to find the kind of crowd you want to go around with.)

Always, between classes, the sweet smell of pot is heavy in the toilets, and you can buy it, as well as stronger stuff, in and around school anytime you want to. Drinking goes on openly in the school parking lot and empty liquor bottles—vodka and pop wines are presently the favorites—and beer cans litter the parking spaces of people who live nearby. Although they do a lot of complaining, it doesn't get them much of anywhere.

Even so, enough kids get busted for one thing or another that Charles isn't taking any risks. Around school, anyway. He hasn't smoked pot since he was twelve and he gets drunk only about twice a year with Jeff Kline, at Jeff's house, when his parents are away. In between, at parties, he drinks a beer or two if it's available.

At various times in his life he has considered being a fireman, a big-league ball player, an astronaut, forest ranger, airplane test pilot, racing car driver, human fly, and international spy. In the last several years, he has leaned toward banking because there are so many things you can do with money.

Charles isn't exactly what you call popular, but a lot of people like him. In the halls between classes, boys punch him and girls say "Hi!" and smile. Mrs. Prunehill, who serves the hot table in the cafeteria, likes him and always gives him an extra-large helping of whatever it is.

Although he isn't the greatest student in the world, he does well enough and with more application could do better. His best subject is Math, his poorest, English. His teachers, with the exception of Mr. Baumgardner, like him because he isn't a smart-ass.

Charles's best friend is Jeff Kline. Jeff, though only a little older than Charles, is taller and heavier. He has lots of curly hair the color of, and rather resembling, a copper scouring pad. Having worked all the summer before on a construction gang, where he made a pile, he doesn't need to work after school. This gives him time for dramatics, at which he's very good, and debating.

Charles does not have a steady girlfriend. But this is not significant, as going steady doesn't seem to be "in" anymore. But whether it is or whether it isn't, enough girls call Charles to provide him with all the social life he has time for. None of these girls who call him turn him on but that's all right. With almost enough money in the bank to buy his car, he is not planning to run the risk of spending any more of it on abortions. For God's sake.

One girl he'd kind of like to go out and have some fun with (within limits) is Lucy Twining. Lucy has pale blue eyes, a large soft mouth, and blonde hair (darker at the roots), a red MG that her parents gave her for her sixteenth birthday, and a not-too-good reputation that she gave herself. He does not think that Lucy would have gotten herself pregnant.

Lucy, however, has interests other than Charles. In fact, until the day before, when she leaned over and whispered that obscene remark about Mr. Baumgardner, she has never said as much as a word to him.

But now, here she is, clattering down the hall after him in a pair of those ridiculous shoes she's always wearing, loudly calling, "Lover boy! What's your hurry?"

As there's no one else in sight, he stops and waits for her to catch up with him. She is a lot taller than Daisy to begin with, and in her weird shoes, she's almost as big as he is. A large skylight is situated just above the spot where they are standing, and in the sun that is streaming in, Charles sees how pale blue her eyes are and that the pupils are contracted almost to nothing.

"If you're not doing anything after school, I'll

drive you home," says Lucy. Her voice is husky, a little coarse, as if she'd yelled too loud or too long at a football game.

Lucy's closeness to him, and the quality of her voice, gives Charles such a feeling of weakness in his kidneys that he mumbles when he says that he's sorry but he has to work.

Lucy pouts, but she does not give up. "Well, then, I'll drive you to work. And if you won't let me do that"—she grins—"I'll drive you crazy." Her fingernails are long, pointed, and covered with a black polish that makes them look as if she had pounded them with a hammer. She squeezes Charles's arm so hard with these talons that he can feel it under his jacket.

While she's still squeezing, a gang of kids comes down the hall toward them and with a "Bye, see ya" she dives into their midst.

Charles likes riding in the open MG next to Lucy Twining. Between stoplights, she drives very fast and brakes suddenly. She makes the tires squeal when she rounds corners. She makes a quick run out to Merrill Park, driving as far as the roadblock, then back again. They arrive in the parking lot of Farley's supermarket with only minutes to spare before Charles must go to work.

As he climbs over the side of the car and says "good-bye," Lucy gives him a narrow look, laughs her hoarse throaty laugh, and says, "Whatever it is that you're doing to yourself, I like it. The funny thing is,

I never even *noticed* you until yesterday. You just look different, somehow."

Charles does not have to reply because Lucy guns the MG out of the parking lot like a racetrack driver.

Inside the store, before he puts on his white apron, he has time to make a quick trip to the men's rest room, employees only.

Fortunately, no one else is in there to see him as he peers at himself in the mirror above the washbowl. He had not thought that being a father would show in his face, but by moving so close that his breath clouds both his glasses and the mirror, he decides that Lucy is right. He *does* look different, and it is not just because he cut himself that morning while shaving. He steps back a few feet and examines himself at a distance. He *does* have a new maturity of bearing. There is a hint of pain about his eyes that shows that he has suffered and that his sleep has been disrupted.

It has all come about since he became the father of a son.

He looks at himself again, raises his chin, examines the cleft, straightens his shoulders, and walks out of the rest room straight into the arms of Mr. Farley, who advises him that he is five minutes late for work.

12
IN A JAM

Charles's mind is elsewhere than on the job at hand. To make matters worse, he is sacking for "Macho" Muriel, who is an American Indian. This is not because he has anything against Indians—when he was a child he longed to be one, once painting his body with iodine and water—but because Muriel looks (and acts) like an Indian *chief,* which, almost anyone will admit, is not so good in a woman. In her white uniform, wearing a button on her chest that says I'M MURIEL, she is roughly the same size and shape as the six-foot, two-inch refrigerator standing in his kitchen at home.

Muriel, however, is more than large. She is the speediest checker in the store, and when he works with her, groceries pile up a lot faster than he can put them in the big brown paper bags that have FARLEY'S—WE SELL FOR LESS BECAUSE IT SAVES YOU MONEY (what this means, no one has ever been able to figure out) printed on them in large black letters.

Moreover, Macho Muriel is always watching him out of the corner of an eye as hard and black as a piece of coal, to see if he puts groceries into the sacks in proper order. There *are* rules, of course, which you learn the first few days. Like, you put heavy things on the bottom of the sack, lighter things next, and fragile things on top. In addition, there are other niceties that the "Big M" likes to see preserved. Packages of meat or chicken that are dripping blood, or any kind of frozen food or damp food, must be sacked separately before going into the big bag.

Since he has come to work this afternoon, he has already been bawled out once by Macho Muriel—and he has the distinct impression that Mr. Farley was in earshot—for putting a dozen extra-large, Grade A eggs in the sack ahead of a number two and a half can of tomatoes.

Now Macho is eating his ass out again. This time, the indiscretion involves the unwise placement of a carton containing three 150-watt, white-light, no-glare, long-life light bulbs in the same sack with three Indian River pink grapefruit. But he scarcely hears her. His mind is recreating the scene in the Elderbury kitchen that morning. It is but one of several scenes that has been harassing him all day.

He does not know exactly how he had expected his mother to act when she came downstairs that morning. Certainly, he didn't expect her to be wearing a scarlet *A* on her striped coverall apron. (For whatever she is, she is *not* an adulteress—actually, he does not even know she was doing anything more than kissing Mr. Bascomb—because she was divorced from his father more years ago than he can remember.) Nor is Mr. Bascomb, at least as far as he knows, an adulterer—he's a widower, his wife having died of cancer three months before. But even so, putting the very best possible complexion on everything, it does seem to Charles when he comes downstairs that morning that his mother's attitude is almost brazen. Not only does she show no sign of guilt, but she makes no kind of explanation. Instead she hums a little tune—something she never does in the morning—as she fixes Charles four strips of bacon, two scrambled eggs, three pieces of toast and places them with the customary accompaniments before him on the kitchen table.

Luckily for him, she is so preoccupied with whatever went on (if anything did) the night before between her and Mr. Bascomb that she does not think to inquire why *he* came home at nine thirty when he was presumably going to spend the evening studying with Jeff Kline.

Macho Muriel brings him back to cold reality when she snaps her fingers—with a sound like a firecracker going off—and tells him to get the dustpan, the kitty litter, and a mop. Charles looks down and sees that he has dropped a jar (large size) of strawberry jam and that a Sargasso Sea of broken glass, syrup, and strawberries is moving toward one of Macho Muriel's incredibly large white oxfords.

As he cleans up the mess, Charles is *positive* Mr. Farley is watching.

Charles does not want to lose his job at Farley's

for several reasons, the most important being that with one, possibly two more paychecks he will have enough money to buy his car. This consideration is enough to make him shape up, and he sacks Muriel's despicable groceries with such tender loving care that not until he's through work at eight o'clock does he have an opportunity to come to grips with his most vexing problem, i.e., does Daisy really mean it when she says she is going to give his baby away?

He thinks she does. She might, he tells himself, do it just to spite him.

He thinks of his baby lying there in the hospital nursery wrapped in swaddling clothes (this expression comes quite naturally to his mind), forever unaware of his parentage, never to know why he was given away. He thinks about himself, never seeing his baby again, never knowing who got him. Never seeing him play championship football or compete in the Olympics or win the British Open. A lump comes into Charles's throat the size of a baseball. There is some smog in the air that makes his eyes sting.

13
SURPRISE!

When Charles gets home from work, Pamela Elderbury has her cutting board laid out on the dining room table and is moving pieces of a dress pattern here and there on some white material covered with green and blue polka dots. She stops humming long enough to ask Charles if he had a good day—to which he replies with a Macho Muriel-type grunt—and to tell him that there is chili con carne in the Crock Pot, pear and cottage cheese salad in the refrigerator, and two Hostess cakes in the bread box.

One good thing about his mother, Charles thinks as he eats, is that she doesn't talk all the time. She makes a few comments about what went on at work if she thinks it will interest him but she doesn't bore in on him the way Bob Borg, who also works at Farley's, says his mother does. She wants to know who he ate lunch with, and who said what to whom, until it gets to the point that Bob doesn't want to tell her anything at all.

Tonight, Charles is especially grateful that his

mother makes no mention of Mr. Bascomb—which makes one less thing to worry about—when she comes out into the kitchen, carrying the scissors in one hand and a flapping piece of paper pattern in the other.

"Oh, Charles," she says. "I almost forgot. You had a telephone call. It came about five thirty, right after I got home. I left the number there on the pad by the telephone."

Charles's plate is clean, his milk glass empty, he belches politely with a hand in front of his mouth. "Better call."

"Not tonight," says his mother. "She won't be in her office until morning. She says to ask for Miss Shrinking."

"Miss *Shrinking*," says Charles, and he belches again, less politely. Nevertheless, he gets up and looks at the number written on the pad. "Doesn't mean anything to me," he says.

"Well, you'll find out in the morning," replies his mother and goes back to cutting out her dress.

Charles, however, cannot put the telephone call out of his mind. He only knows that, whoever Miss Shrinking is, he does not want to talk to her—and that if he can help it, he is not going to.

He is hardly out of bed the next morning, however, before his mother reminds him. "That Miss Shrinking," she says, in loud clear tones, "said that she would be in her office early this morning. By seven thirty."

Five minutes later, Pamela Elderbury says, "If you don't call that Miss Shrinking before you go to school, you won't get a chance."

The telephone is in the front hall, and as Charles walks toward it like a condemned man, his mother goes to the kitchen with the air of one who has no interest in the conversation about to take place and would not listen even if she were in the same room.

Charles dials the number as soon as he hears the sound of water running in the kitchen sink. The voice on the other end of the wire says, "Allied Social Service Agency," in decibels that are audible only to his own ears.

In muted tones, he asks to speak to Miss Shrinking and has only to wait a moment before there is an answer.

Charles identifies himself, then says "yes," "no," "he thinks so," and the conversation is over.

Pamela Elderbury comes to the kitchen door and looks out into the hall. She does not want to ask Charles about the phone call, but she cannot restrain herself. She says artfully, "Who was it, dear?"

Charles, who has not yet placed the phone back on the cradle, stares into the black mouthpiece. There is no time to think of an answer, so he says, "Surprise." It is the first thing that comes into his mind, but it satisfies Pamela Elderbury.

"Charles," she says with a giddy laugh. "Now don't be foolish. I don't want you spending your hard-earned money on *me*. I couldn't ask for a better surprise for my birthday than a good report card."

Surprise, Charles thinks hollowly. *Some surprise.*

14
FLOPPING

The one good thing that comes out of his conversation with the woman at the Allied Social Services Agency is that it alerts him to the fact that he has not only forgotten all about his mother's birthday, but he cannot remember when it is.

Otherwise, all is disaster. He tells Lucy Twining, who pounces on him just as he is going into Mr. Baumgardner's class, to "cool it." (For the time being, he has had his fill of women.) Lucy tells him to go suck. He bombs in a trick quiz concocted by Miss Fritz in American Government, and stands at the blackboard like an idiot when Mr. Baylor asks him to work a problem in Trig that he ordinarily could have worked with his eyes shut. In track he falls over the first hurdle he comes to.

With every ounce of his being, with every fiber

of his brain, he is gearing himself toward the meeting he is to have that afternoon after school with Miss Shrinking in the Parents' Conference Room at the Hospital of the Immaculate Conception.

What can Miss Shrinking want of him?

The worst possible thing that he can imagine is that she will demand that he marry Daisy. Even to keep his baby, he is not willing to do this. (It is not, he tells himself, as if he had ever *really* loved Daisy. Or she him. It was just one of those things. Not that it wasn't great—after all these months his stick gets hard even thinking about it—but with the geographical distance that separated them, with Daisy's father keeping her practically a prisoner, plus all the lies *he* had to tell (and no place to go after he told them except to a raft in the middle of Lake Larkspur), things finally got too complicated. They'd both agreed on that.

Even if he and Daisy should marry and get a divorce immediately afterward, the very thought of marriage is intolerable. Who wants to be married and divorced before he is seventeen?

15
BIG AND STRONG

Although Miss Shrinking has not asked him to meet her at the hospital until after school—she has suggested four o'clock—Charles cuts his last class of the day so he won't miss the afternoon showing.

City buses run with maddening slowness and it is almost three o'clock when Charles gets to the maternity floor. By then the big push at the viewing window is about over. The only people remaining are two middle-aged women of about forty and an older man who are looking at a baby being held up to the window. It is the most miserable-looking specimen of a baby Charles has ever seen.

Charles thinks that the three must share his opinion, for none of them is "ooooohing" or "ahing." They do not say anything at all. Instead, they step back from the window to make way for Charles, who is gratified that the nursery nurse recognizes him, and immediately goes away and comes back with his baby.

The baby has grown since Charles last saw him, which is less than forty-eight hours ago.

This time, the baby's eyes are open. A deep, dark blue (like his own), they look directly at him. To Charles, they seem filled with ancient wisdom. The nose is short and straight, the ears are set tightly to his head, and the lips are smiling. The cleft in the chin is more pronounced than ever.

Charles hears a chuckle behind him. It is the elderly gentleman. "Look at the size of those hands," he tells the two ladies. "You can tell he is going to be a big fellow, all right."

"Yes!" adds one of the ladies. "Big *and* strong." She draws attention to the size of the baby's feet, which he is kicking out from his blanket.

Charles, who up to this moment has not looked at either his baby's hands or feet, now does so. He finds that what these more experienced observers have said is true.

But that is not all. He has already come to a conclusion of his own. In this baby there is no trace of Daisy at all. From head to foot, from the cleft in his chin to the size of his feet—the tattered sneakers Charles is wearing are size twelve—his baby is every inch an Elderbury.

16
POWER

Charles has to ask where the Parents' Conference Room is.

Miss Shrinking and Daisy are already there. Daisy is wearing what looks to be a man's bathrobe many sizes too big for her and scuffs that are likewise too big. Also, since he saw her last, she has cut her hair. It is about ten thousand different lengths, all short, and makes her look like a boy except, of course, for her chest, which even under the voluminous bathrobe shows that she is a girl.

He notices these things as Miss Shrinking rises to meet him. "So you're *Charles!*" she says. She sounds surprised, as if he's not what she had expected him to be at all.

Charles, however, is also surprised. She does not resemble a social worker at all. (He has only a vague idea of what a social worker *is*.)

Miss Shrinking wears large black glasses that are as big around as water tumblers—his own glasses are quite large—and is considerably younger than his mother, who will be, he thinks, thirty-eight on the birthday that is soon to take place. Her hair is dark brown, smooth, and worn just below her ears. She doesn't have her eyelids covered with a lot of blue-green gook and she has a nice smile.

"You've no idea how glad I am we found you," she says, and points to a chair across from the couch she is sitting on. "Daisy, dear, don't you want to move in a little closer?"

Daisy says she is all right where she is.

Miss Shrinking is not put off by this remark, which is spoken in a rather rude tone of voice, but continues with a little smile. "We might not have found you at all, you know, if it had not been for Miss Purvis. You may have met her. She's the head nurse here on the maternity floor."

Daisy says that is not all Miss Purvis is, and describes it.

Miss Shrinking goes on as if Daisy hasn't said anything. "To make a long story short, Miss Purvis asked Sally Graybar, the Candy Striper who happened to be pushing the gift cart, if she knew the boy who'd been hanging around the nursery. And she did! It seems she goes to your school. Now isn't that a coincidence?"

Charles does not respond, but sinks lower in his chair. He feels his gut contract as Miss Shrinking delves in the briefcase beside her and takes out a manila folder. "Now," she says, "for the baby's family. I know that's what you *really* want to hear about."

Charles is so certain that Miss Shrinking is about to demand that he marry Daisy that he has forgotten about the threat of the baby's adoption.

The words "baby's family" fill him with dread. He does not want to hear anything about them. His baby could be adopted by the president of the United States and it would make no difference to him. If he were declared the heir of all the Rockefellers, it would not make his loss any easier to bear.

Charles does his best not to listen, but in spite of well-developed powers to tune out anything in which he is not interested, certain salient facts seep through.

"Father X," as Miss Shrinking calls him, is an industrial engineer. And "Mother X" is a *nurse*. She has had four miscarriages and now can never have a baby of her own. As a couple, the Xs are highly respected in the community. Although they are not wealthy, they have sufficient income to see that the child growing up will have the usual advantages and, of course, receive a college education. Father X has a Ph.D., and Mother X has a Phi Beta Kappa key.

Charles is silent.

"You may be sure that they have been *thoroughly* investigated and have waited for a baby for a long, long time. And, of course, we follow each case for a year or more to be sure that everything is going as it should."

Miss Shrinking puts the folder away, takes out a sheet of white paper with a lot of printing on it, lays it on the table before Charles, and smiles reassuringly. "I

73

know you will want to read the release through before you sign, and naturally I'll be glad to answer any questions you care to ask."

Charles drops the ball-point pen the social worker hands him and has to get down on his hands and knees to find it. When he picks up the paper with the printing, the words run together in a continuous blur. The only thing he can read on it is Daisy's signature at the bottom of the page, which is written in a script as bold and black as John Hancock's leading off as the first signer of the Declaration of Independence.

Daisy watches him like a hawk as he tries to read.

Miss Shrinking, however, looks quite relaxed. She lights a cigarette. "It is a *much* more satisfactory arrangement," she says, "now that fathers are consulted about their babys' future. In all the cases that I've handled, they have been most reasonable.

Charles scarcely hears her.

Miss Shrinking goes on, "Before the Supreme Court ruling in 1972, the unmarried mother had *complete* control over the baby, which was, of course, *grossly* unfair to the father. Fortunately, society now recognizes that the man has as much potential to care about his child as a woman does."

Daisy, from her corner, interjects a coarse hyphenated expletive pertaining to bulls which Miss Shrinking ignores. "So that is why, Charles," she continues, "we were so happy to locate you. With Daisy's reluctance—actually, I should say refusal—to name the father of the baby, we would have been obliged to go through the laborious process of publication hoping to turn you up, all of which holds up the proceedings."

Charles looks up from the typed page he holds in his hand. His eyes are beginning to clear. He feels as if an electric fan has been turned on inside his head. "You mean," he says slowly, "that if I don't sign this paper the X people can't adopt the baby?"

"That is right, Charles," says Miss Shrinking. There is a new terse note in her voice. "It is the law. Although there are those who think that the rulings have given fathers too much leeway, enabling them to exercise control over both mother and child, I do not subscribe to this view. I simply do not believe for a moment that you would take advantage of your legal right and deny your baby a wonderful home, just to spite Daisy."

"I wouldn't take advantage of it to spite Daisy," says Charles. Very carefully, he lays the pen and paper back on the table. "It's just that I don't feel like signing this paper right now."

Daisy screams three times. It is like the blast of a high-pitched factory whistle.

Two nurses come running and take her away.

BOOK TWO

That shabby corner of God's
allotment where He lets the
nettles grow, and where all
unbaptized infants, notorious
drunkards, suicides and others
of the conjecturably damned
are laid.
—Thomas Hardy, *Tess of the D'Urbervilles*

1

A PIECE OF TIME

It is after five thirty when Charles gets home. His mother is not yet there and he is glad of the respite. It has been, he thinks, as he throws himself down on the sofa, the most emotionally exhausting afternoon of his life. But painful as it is, he reviews it.

After the nurses take Daisy away, Miss Shrinking almost talks an arm off him. First, she goes over once again all the marvelous qualifications of the X family. Then she paints a picture of Daisy that would draw tears from a stone. Poor Daisy—who had to drop out of school before the end of the first semester! (Miss Shrinking asks Charles rather pointedly if he had known Daisy was an almost straight-A student, and Charles said he had not.) Poor Daisy—who a year from now will not be able to graduate with the rest of her class! Poor Daisy—whose disgrace is known to all the school! Poor Daisy—whose home life is intolerable!

In her zeal, Miss Shrinking verbally italicizes all the key words. It is *brave* of Daisy to do the *hard* thing and *have* the baby when the *easy* thing would have been to have an *abortion*.

Charles is, in truth, moved by these arguments, but he does his best not to show it. For the first time since he has been plunged into the middle of this whole miserable affair, he is holding the baby's future in his hands. To every argument that Miss Shrinking presents, he repeats doggedly that he has to have time to think, that he must have time to see if he can work something *out*.

Miss Shrinking finally agrees that he does, indeed, have this right and that it is part of the new philosophy—she doesn't sound quite as crazy about the new philosophy as she did—that men, indeed, have as much potential to care about their children as women do. She insists, however, that she and Charles keep in touch. *Closely* in touch. She gives Charles two phone numbers—her office number, which he already has, and the other at her home address.

All that he has really accomplished is to buy a piece of time.

Lying there on the sofa, Charles's stomach makes a series of plaintive noises, rather like the sound of an infant wailing. Charles knows it comes from hunger. He is starving, and there is still no sign of his mother.

He goes to the kitchen and looks in the Crock Pot. It is cold. There is no note on the refrigerator telling him that there is a pizza in the freezer. Nor is there anything *in* the refrigerator that is ready to eat without preparation.

The phone rings as he peers into the empty cookie jar.

It is his mother. She says, "Charles, is that you?"

Charles says, "Yes," in a hollow voice.

"Dear," she says. From her voice, Charles can tell there is someone in the same room with her.

"I'm working late tonight," she says, "to accommodate Mr. Bascomb. Later this evening he's flying to Washington for a meeting with the Interstate Commerce Commission. In fact, Mr. Bascomb is here in the office with me now. We'll have some sandwiches sent in presently, to tide us over. I should be home about ten."

That is all she says. There is no mention of what he is to eat. No mention of anything, really, except the loathsome Mr. Bascomb.

Charles fixes himself two peanut butter sandwiches and pours a glass of milk, which he takes with him into the living room. Only one thing lightens his gloom and that is the certain knowledge that it would have been wrong to sign the release for the adoption until every possibility for keeping his baby is exhausted.

2
FAMILY ALBUM

Charles thinks wistfully of the father he has never known. Although he has always *missed* his father, not until the last few days does he realize how much he has missed him. (Ironically, he had even thought he was happy!) He does not even have a decent picture of his father. To his knowledge, the only one in existence is in his baby book, which is kept in a cupboard under the bookcases that line one end of the living room.

Although he had loved looking at his baby book as a child, it is years since he even thought of it. He gets it out. It is a loose-leaf affair, covered in a nursery print material and held together with silk cord. Pasted on the inside front cover is his birth certificate. Across from it, in neat lettering (his mother's) there is printed CHARLES PENROSE ELDERBURY. HIS BOOK. On the next page is his footprint. He stares at it, examining the intricate whorls, and for a moment is lost in wonder that that foot has now grown to the size of the one presently occupying the coffee table.

The rest of the book is made up of snapshots. Although a few have come loose, most are still pasted in and beneath each is a legend in his mother's hand. CHARLES AT THREE WEEKS; CHARLES AT TWO MONTHS; CHARLES EATING CEREAL. (More cereal is on the outside of his mouth than in.) There is a photograph of his mother, so young and pretty he scarcely recognizes her, holding him in her arms. (He examines this picture of himself with special care.)

He skips over a half dozen pages of pictures taken when they lived with his Grandmother Penrose—that was while his mother was going back to college to get her degree and learning shorthand and typing so she'd be sure to get a job—and before they moved to this present house where most of his important memories begin. He still has not come to the picture of his father. He wonders if something could have happened to it. He does not, however, suspect his mother. He has never heard her speak unkindly of his father. (He scarcely has heard her speak of him at all.)

At last, he finds the snapshot he is looking for. He moves the baby book a little closer to a table lamp in order to see it better. (He observes it has no legend under it.) In the picture, he is bundled in a snow suit and is sitting on a tricycle which is far too big for him. His feet, clad in overshoes, do not come anywhere near the pedals. Bending over him from behind, his hands on the tricycle's handlebars, and looking up directly at the camera, is this splendid man. Although it is winter, the man is bare-headed. He wears no outer coat or jacket, only a V-necked sweater over an open-throated shirt. He is squinting a little against the sun, but he is smiling. There is a cleft in his chin.

Charles feels the muscles in his throat tighten. He knows—or admits to himself for the first time—that his father is dead. There can be no other explanation why his father has never come to see him or made any inquiry about him.

If I allow *my* baby to be given away, Charles thinks, when he is my age, what will he think about *me?*"

A moment later the overhead garage door comes down with a bang. It is after eleven o'clock, and Charles's mother is home. At last. He quickly puts the baby book back in the cupboard. When Pamela Elderbury comes in, Charles is reading the evening paper. He thinks his mother looks flustered.

"Charles!" she says. "I didn't think you'd still be up! You have to be at work tomorrow morning at eight o'clock, you know."

"I know," he says. "But I have to talk to you. About my father."

"Your *father!*" She finishes hanging up her coat in the hall closet and then comes back into the room. "What brings up your father at this hour of the night?"

Charles says he doesn't know. He just wants to talk about him, that's all.

"I think it could wait until morning," says

Pamela Elderbury. She smothers a yawn with one hand and then tucks in a strand of hair that has escaped from her chignon and hangs in the shape of a limp S at the back of her neck.

"Mom, *please?*"

Pamela Elderbury sighs. "O.K., Sweetie," she says. "What is it you want to know?"

"What kind of a man," asks Charles, "*was* my father, anyway?"

3
SOMEWHERE OUT THERE

It is impossible for Charles's mother to tell her son what kind of a man his father was or what he was like. Still, she tries. But it takes her some time to start.

"Well," she says at last, "he liked the outdoors."

This sounds all right to Charles, who says, "Go on."

"And he was terribly good-looking, and funny, and he had so much personality he could charm the birds right out of the trees." She looks faintly wistful as she adds, "He might have liked to be an explorer or, if he'd lived in another day, a crusader—not that he believed very much in anything." She says this without criticism. "But he was never around when I needed him. And when he was around, I couldn't afford him."

"Like . . . like . . ." Charles swallows. "Like he wasn't around when I was born?"

"Well, yes." She looks off into space as if she sees Charles's father out there somewhere. "He liked to fish and climb mountains and hunt, and he liked the best of everything to do it with . . ."

"Did he . . . ?" Charles begins, then pauses, not knowing exactly how to say what he wants to say. "Did he, I mean . . . did he finally just go *off?*"

"No, not really." (Charles knows his mother is trying to be fair.) "He told me he was leaving, that he might not be back. And that I should get a divorce. He knew it was the best for everybody."

"Except for *me*. He couldn't have liked *me* very much." It hurts him to say this. He expects his mother to deny it, and she does.

"No," she says, "it wasn't that way at all. After the divorce, I think he would have liked to come back to see you . . . if he could."

"Did . . . did he die?"

Pamela Elderbury gets up abruptly. "Charles," she says, "you are asking me impossible questions. Questions for which I have no answer."

And that is all he gets out of her.

4

THE SCENT OF APPLE BLOSSOMS

Mr. Farley waylays Charles as he comes in the door of the supermarket the next morning. He says that he has been observing him, that there are a number of boys his age who would like to work for Farley's —there is a long waiting list—and if he does not shape up he is through. Charles says he will try to do better.

Luckily, he is not assigned to sack for Macho Muriel but for Hubert Turnquist, who is Mr. Farley's nephew and not a great deal older than Charles. Hubert came to work at Farley's right out of high school and is learning the business. A tall, thin young man who, in profile, looks rather like a turtle, he sometimes works as a checker. Other times he works in produce, bakery goods, or behind the Courtesy Counter.

This morning, Hubert has returned to work after taking part of his vacation. He has been home helping his wife, Audrey, take care of their new baby, born a little over a week ago. The baby is a boy, and Hubert is handing out cigars. Although Charles does not smoke, he takes a cigar. It seems only fitting that he should do so. (He thinks, possibly, later that day he may try it.) He also wishes there were some way he could bring up the subject of *his* baby. Each hour, each day that passes, the desire is growing in him to tell somebody. Even working with Hubert Turnquist, however, helps his mental condition—there is this hidden bond —and he works overtime without complaint even though it means he won't get to see the baby until the evening showing.

He picks up his paycheck, cashes it, and, in an unwonted burst of spending, buys a blue glass container filled with Apple Blossom bath salts—the container may be used later for a vase—for Daisy, and a child-sized football with ink lacing printed on it, for the baby. He thinks that bringing these gifts may soften Daisy up when he pleads with her to keep the baby. He is prepared to offer financial assistance, if necessary. (But not too much.)

Even with his mother's car, however—he thinks she let him take it because of guilt—it is after five o'clock when he gets to the hospital. Already there is the clatter of dishes and silverware on the maternity floor in preparation for the serving of the evening meal. He gets off the elevator and slopes off down the corridor. He hopes no one will see him and make him leave before he gets to Daisy's room, visiting hours being long since over. But no one does. Holding the gifts before him like a shield, he opens the door.

He says Daisy's name softly and then freezes. There is a fat woman in her bed! The women in the other three beds are strangers, too. All look at him curiously as he hastily backs out.

A nurse Charles has not seen before is seated behind the counter at the central nursing station. "Daisy Dallinger," he croaks. "Where is she?"

The nurse, who is writing something, does not look up. "Ms. Dallinger," she says, "was released yesterday. Patients are confined for only four and a half days if the delivery is normal."

Confined and released, Charles thinks. The place sounds more like a penitentiary or a lunatic asylum than a hospital. Charles clenches his larynx. "The baby . . . did the baby go home with her?"

"That I cannot say," says the nurse, still writing. "That is privileged information."

Charles stumbles off down the hall, bumps into an orderly pushing an empty hospital cart. At the same time there is a sound of breaking glass and the strong scent of apple blossoms mingles with the already unappetizing smell of the evening meal.

5
INDIGO

Once before when Charles had had his mother's car—he had told her he was going to a movie with Jeff Kline—he had driven Daisy home. He let her out a quarter of a block away because she'd lied, too, and was afraid her father would see her coming home with a boy. She pointed out the house, however, as they drove past. It's the one, she said, with all the junk in the front yard. She added that when her father did anything at all, he sold spare parts from old cars he salvaged.

Charles recognizes Daisy's house. Its front yard is still filled with miscellaneous car parts.

It takes a good deal of courage to go up to the front door and knock, and even then he is praying, really praying, that Daisy will be the one to appear and that she will be carrying his baby.

The door is quickly opened.

It is almost as if the man, whom Charles recognizes at once as Daisy's father, has been waiting for him. He is wearing dirty overalls over a long-sleeved (also dirty) suit of underwear. In one hand he holds a quart of Miller High Life. With the other hand he is scratching his belly.

"Is Daisy in?" asks Charles in a voice he does not recognize.

Daisy's father belches. He says, "No!" in a bellow that would do justice to a lion in the Cedar City Zoo. "Daisy is not in, and she's not going to be in. I'll not have a whore living in *my* house with her runny-nosed bastard kid."

He shuts the door, only to open it again before Charles can move away.

"And who are you, is it, that is wantin' to know?" Although this is a fake Irish accent that Daisy's father is using, it is none the less terrible for all of that. "If I iver get me hands on the one who violated me little girrl, he'll wish that he has never been borrrn."

Charles hears this latter remark from a distance. Already, he is running toward his car, which, deliberately, he has parked some distance away. When he reaches it he is met by a miniature Daisy with a yellow canvas bag, filled with neatly folded copies of *The Cedar City Evening Tribune,* which she is wearing with the strap around her forehead like a headband. She is so small and the bag is so heavy that she is almost bent double. She raises her head to speak to him.

"I'm Indigo," she says. "Daisy's sister. But if you're looking for Daisy, she's at my Aunt Nelda's. Dad kicked her out. Kicked Daisy out, I mean."

Charles is so horrified at this information that

91

his voice cracks. "And your . . . your Aunt Nelda, where does she live?"

"Over by the Parkway Shopping Center," says the child. "In that big brown house that's sort of left over like, on the corner of Parkway and Holbrook, next to the car wash before you get to the traffic lights. It's been made into apartments," she adds, as if she is in some way gently breaking the news.

"Thanks," says Charles huskily. He is thinking that, although Daisy's father is terrible, *Mrs.* Dallinger must be very nice to have given her babies names like Indigo and Daisy. He is wishing with all his heart that he had something to give this little girl with the indigo eyes, but he has nothing except the toy football, which does not seem appropriate.

Indigo, however, is not willing to let him go. She transfixes him with eyes of transcending blueness and says, "I'll bet you're the one. I'll just bet anything you are." Then wisely adds, as if agreeing with herself, "Daisy *told* me you were cute."

6
NO PLACE FOR A BABY

Indigo's instructions are precise and Charles finds the brown house without difficulty. It is a big house and it is easy to see that once it was very fine. A porch runs around three sides of it. There are a number of little railed balconies, all a little tipsy, a turret shaped like a plump Roman candle, and several stained glass windows in which the last rays of spring sunshine are caught in a prism of light.

In one of the downstairs windows there is a sign reading FURNISHED APARTMENT TO LET, and up one side of the house itself a rather crude wooden staircase rises, giving access to what was once the attic.

Charles parks the Toyota behind a pick-up truck and goes up the walk. There is no doorbell to ring. Inside, the hallway is so dark that he has difficulty reading the names on the dog-eared calling cards and scraps of paper which are tacked to the various closed doors. None has the first name of Nelda.

He takes a staircase with an ornate balustrade to the second floor. Here again he has no luck until he gets to the very back of the house, where he finds a hand-lettered card that reads MS. NELDA SOPOFORIS.

He knocks, then hears a gentle scurrying. The door opens about six inches on a safety chain, showing a slice of Daisy's face. With its fringe of dark hair around it, it is as pale as a new moon.

"You haven't signed it yet, have you?" says Daisy in a flat voice.

"No," says Charles. Looking over Daisy's head, he can see a sink, a daybed, and a card table with a pile of what looks to be schoolbooks. Another smaller, darker room lies beyond. "I just . . ."

Daisy gives him a hostile look. "If you haven't signed it, I don't want to talk to you," she says, and before he can even argue with her, she closes the door.

Charles turns away.

Down on the street he gives the football to a snotty-nosed little kid who is riding a tricycle up and down the sidewalk. From what he has seen of the place where Daisy lives with her Aunt Nelda, it doesn't seem to him to be any place to raise a baby. He is almost glad not to find him there.

7
LOVERBIRD

Charles's mother has not waited to have dinner with him, as she is going to a civic music concert with a friend who is picking her up at seven thirty. She has been worried about Charles, she says, and wants to know where in the world he has been.

He tells her he had to work overtime at Mr. Farley's request, which is in part the truth. He is finding that the more he lies or stretches the truth, the more expert he becomes.

He eats dinner morosely—baked beans and sausage from the Crock Pot—under the watchful eye of his mother, who has set up the ironing board in the kitchen and is pressing the dress she plans to wear.

She asks him if he feels all right.

He says he does.

"You don't think you have a temperature, do you?" She stands the iron on end and comes over to him, putting the back of her fingers to his forehead. Charles jerks his head away and says he's already told her once he feels O.K.

"Well, there's no need to bite my head off," she says reasonably. The telephone rings and she goes off to answer it.

When she comes back she says, "It's for you. A girl. I don't recognize the voice."

Charles says "hello" cautiously, as there is the possibility that the call is from Miss Shrinking, but it turns out to be Lucy Twining, who is not sore at him after all.

"Hi, Loverbird," she says. "I hope your disposition is better than it was the last time I spoke to you. Is it?"

Charles replies that he doesn't know whether it is or not.

"You do play hard to get, don't you?" says Lucy cheerfully. "But I *like* you that way. It brings out all my feral, feminine instincts—if you know what 'feral' means. Anyway, if you're not doing anything tonight, why don't you come on over? My immature parents are going out for fun and games so I'm having some kids in."

Charles tightens his tonsils and says he can't come as he is going to be busy. This is the truth. For just at that moment he remembers that Jeff Kline has asked him over to his house to spend the night. Jeff's parents are also going out for fun and games and Jeff has to stay home and baby-sit with his two-year-old brother, Joey.

Lucy takes the refusal with good grace, and says she'll get him yet.

96

When Charles returns to the kitchen, his mother wants to know who it was on the phone.

"Just some tart," says Charles in a sour voice.

Pamela Elderbury says she is shocked and that Charles should be ashamed of himself for talking that way about one of his friends, and a girl at that. "Besides," she adds, "I didn't know you were going to Jeff's to spend the night."

Charles says he just forgot to tell her, that's all.

"Well," she says, forgiving him, "if you're sure you feel all right."

8
JEFF'S HOUSE

Jeff Kline's house is almost as familiar to Charles as his own is. Over the years he has spent a lot of time there. (Jeff's mother, a large woman with a soft bosom and a hearty manner—all of her children are grown except Jeff and Joey, who was not, she says, "on the drawing board"—encourages it.)

The Klines have always had the best place in the neighborhood to play. There is a basketball hoop fastened to the front of the barn. (Though part of it is used as a garage, it really *is* a barn and the house was once a farmhouse, the city growing up around it.) In the side yard, there's a softball diamond, a place to pitch horseshoes, and a bag swing that flies you out over a gully. Behind the barn there is a meadow as big as half a city block where he and Jeff used to pitch their tents and pretend they were sleeping in the wilderness.

Charles walks over to Jeff's house.

Mr. and Mrs. Kline have already left for wherever it is they are going. Jeff is upstairs trying to get his little brother Joey, who is running around without any clothes on, into bed.

Joey is practicing somersaults and peers out at Charles from between his fat legs, saying, "Ook! Ookadoey!"

Jeff translates. "He's saying, 'Look at Joey.' He's only two, you know."

Charles, who has not seen Joey for some time, looks at him with new interest. For Joey is a cute little boy with hard, red-apple cheeks and blue eyes. His bottom has deep dimples in it, and his wiener isn't as long as the first joint of Charles's little finger and about as big around as a piece of elbow macaroni. Charles thinks his baby's wiener must be really small and wishes he could see it.

Jeff finally catches up with Joey, throws him down on the floor with a kind of knee lock, gets a double-diaper arrangement on him, and then fastens him into some kind of a little suit with feet in it, a

98

crotch that snaps, and a zipper up the front. This is all accomplished with such ease that Charles marvels.

"Are babies ... little kids ... a lot of work?" Charles asks casually.

"Naw," says Jeff, putting Joey in his crib. He turns out the light and says to Charles, "Come on. He'll settle down in a minute."

9
DRINKING

They go downstairs and sit in the porch swing, although it is still a little cold to be comfortable outdoors.

It is a perfect time, Charles thinks, to tell Jeff about his baby but he does not know how to begin.

Jeff speaks first. "My folks aren't going to be home until God knows when. How about a little something to drink?"

"Like what?"

"I don't know 'like what.' They had a party last weekend. Why don't we see what's lying around that can be spared?"

They go to the kitchen.

Mr. Kline does not keep his liquor locked up. (He believes, according to Jeff, that if a kid is going to drink, he's going to drink. That he'll get it one way or another.) So all the booze is in the bottom cupboard next to the wax paper, plastic wrap, and sandwich bags.

While Jeff is taking all the various bottles out of the cupboard and putting them on the kitchen floor, Joey makes a trip downstairs. Jeff makes him go upstairs again by himself. He tells Charles that Joey is just testing him to see if he can get away with anything.

To Charles, the rearing of children appears to grow easier and easier, if one just knows how.

Jeff finally selects five bottles: a half-gallon jug of Christian Brothers Burgundy which is slightly less than half full, a bottle of Old Grand-dad bourbon within two inches of the top, a gallon jug of Popov vodka that has barely been tapped, a bottle of Almadén Chablis which is slightly more than three-fourths full, and a better than half a fifth of a light Jamaican rum. Jeff decants what he hopes is an unnoticeable amount from each bottle into five empty glass jars that once held peanut butter. He fills an ice bucket, gets two clean glasses, and tells Charles that they will take this stuff down to his room.

Jeff's room is really the basement. He has all of it, except the space devoted to the furnace, hot water heater, and his mother's washing machine and dryer, and it is really fixed up nice.

Charles loves Jeff's room, but what he loves most about it is the water bed which Jeff inherited from one of his older brothers, who had the room before him and no longer lives at home. Charles settles himself on the water bed and Jeff, who has arranged himself on the floor with the liquor before him, asks Charles what he would like to have.

Charles selects the Burgundy. It is not a matter for any great consideration to him—or to Jeff, either—because he knows that sooner or later they are going to drink all of it.

With the water sloshing gently beneath him, Charles feels more at peace than he has at any time since learning he is a father. He and Jeff have been through a lot together. He remembers the night Jeff asked him about Rh. Jeff is worried sick because he has just accidentally learned that he was an "Rh baby." He wonders if this means that either his mother or father had a venereal disease at the time of his birth.

Charles does not know, but he sympathizes with Jeff's fears that it may affect his reproductive life. He undertakes to find out, and does, from his Grandmother Penrose, to whom he puts the question directly. "Rh," he says, "what is it?"

Charles and Jeff, over the years, have had many enlightening conversations about subjects relating to sex—in the main, this was before the sex counselor came to Cedar City Junior High—that perplexed them. Like, what's the world's biggest prick measurement? Is something wrong if you have one testicle lower than the other? Or which way should your stick curve when it's hard? Once Charles asked Jeff if he thinks he should

101

let his mother know he's having wet dreams and Jeff, with great wisdom, said he didn't think it's necessary and let it go at that.

Now, looking back, it seems to Charles that, at the time, he and Jeff were pretty stupid about a lot of things. Still, they weren't the only ones. One kid told the counselor that what he'd like to know is how much parents think kids really know.

Charles clears his throat. Yes, he thinks. If he's going to tell anyone about having a baby, Jeff is the one.

When he finally gets it all out, Jeff puts down his glass of whatever it is, and says, "Lord, God Almighty."

Not until Jeff says this does Charles remember that Jeff is a Catholic and might well regard having a baby when you're not married as a sin.

Whether he does or whether he doesn't, there's no doubt that he is shaken. "Whose?" he says at last.

"Why, mine," says Charles.

"Stupid!" says Jeff, hitting his forehead. "I don't mean *that*. Who *had* it?"

Charles hesitates. "No one you know. She doesn't even go to CCHS. I met her way last summer at Lake Larkspur. She's this girl you let me borrow your car to go out and see a couple of times."

"I hope you didn't do it in my *car*," says Jeff, sounding as if the car had been contaminated.

"No," replies Charles. "On the raft."

Jeff seems mollified by this answer and listens

while Charles explains what a nuisance it all was, having to take your clothes off, swim out to the raft, and then swim back and put your clothes on again, but what with the park police and all, it was the best place they had.

Jeff pours himself a light Jamaican rum and, giving Charles the rest of the bourbon, asks if this girl had one of those hymen things.

When Charles says he thinks she did, Jeff looks down his nose and says, "That makes it worse"—a remark that could be taken several ways—and begins shooting questions like a district attorney on TV. This is another one of Jeff's skills, being able to imitate anybody he wants to. A drunk, Elvis Presley, Henry Kissinger, anybody. He's really good at it and plans to go to acting school if his folks don't put up too much of a fight.

Now, however, Jeff is asking questions for real, but Charles doesn't care. He finds it a relief to talk. He tells Jeff everything. Or practically everything. He thinks he had better keep quiet about giving Daisy the money for an abortion.

Jeff wants to know what Charles is going to do. Charles does not know. Jeff says he will do everything in his power to help. They shake hands, drink the last of the liquor, and weave their way upstairs to the kitchen, bumping into each other, each cautioning the other to be quiet. They rinse out their drinking glasses and the jars that held the liquor and put them in the dishwasher, stumble downstairs again, and fall into the water bed.

103

Sometime later, Mr. and Mrs. Kline come home. The house is quiet. Mr. Kline says he would like a glass of milk with some bourbon whiskey in it for a nightcap and Mrs. Kline says she would like the same.

In the kitchen, while Mrs. Kline takes a carton of milk from the refrigerator, Mr. Kline gets out the bourbon and holds it up to the light, then similarly inspects a number of other liquor bottles on the bottom shelf of the cupboard.

He grins. "Hey, Tess," he says. "I know a couple of kids who are going to have one big head tomorrow morning."

10
LORD HEAR OUR PRAYER

No comment is made when Charles and Jeff come up for breakfast. Mrs. Kline makes pancakes for them until the batter runs out. (For Joey, she makes little ones about the size of a silver dollar and last of all a "pancake man.") Mr. Kline comes in and talks to them.

Mr. and Mrs. Kline have been to early Mass at St. Mary's, but Jeff goes to the ten o'clock Mass at the

University of Cedar City Newman Center. There he plays his Gibson twelve-string folk guitar in company with a girl named Dorita who plays a bass violin a good deal bigger than she is, and two other guys who play guitar, one a Yamaha acoustical and the other a Goya classical.

Charles goes to Newman Mass with Jeff a couple of times a year, usually after he's stayed all night. (At Mass, he doesn't join in—though he does rather like it —but just sits there like a spectator at a sporting event that somebody gave him a free ticket to.)

This Sunday, though, the music is unusually good—Jeff has told him it would be—and when the group plays a couple of songs from *Godspell* it gets to him to the point that when the priest, who's almost as long and lanky as "Bird" Fidrych, asks if anyone in the congregation has any petitions they would like to offer, Charles finds himself saying that he'd like to pray (something he hasn't done since he was five years old) for a friend who's got this terrible problem and doesn't know what to do.

This is the very kind of thing the congregation likes to pray for, because each person has in his own mind an idea of what the problem might be, and there is a booming response of "Lord hear our prayer" all around him, which is very satisfying.

Pretty soon it is time to sing again, and as the music soars around him, Charles, without really intending to, once again stands up and, looking down at the song sheet in his hand, joins in.

When I was broke without a dime
And having such a hard, hard time
I didn't need it, 'cause your love could carry me.
And when a friend was doin' bad
I could share all that I had.
I didn't need it, 'cause your love could carry me.

Then comes the chorus, and he's really with it:

Carry me, carry me,
Said I know your love
Is gonna carry me.

Charles is almost sorry Mass is over.

Jeff drops Charles off at home. His mother isn't there, but she's left a note for him. Mr. Bascomb has returned from Washington, D.C.—his meeting was canceled—and he has come by to fill her in on what happened. She will be back, she thinks, no later than five P.M. There are chicken and noodles in the Crock Pot, gelatin salad in the refrigerator, and some Pepperidge Farm apple turnovers in the deep freeze.

11
SUSPENDED

Jeff drives Charles to the Allied Social Services building after school the next day. It is in a kind of crummy part of town but there is, at least, off-street parking. Jeff says he will wait.

Charles dreads this visit with Miss Shrinking almost as much as he feared the first one, but he is afraid that if he doesn't go to see her voluntarily she will call him at home again, a contingency to be avoided at all costs. For things are not at all good at home, Charles having refused to come downstairs and meet Mr. Bascomb the previous afternoon when he and Charles's mother returned from their outing.

At first, she just calls up to him in her musical voice and asks him to come down. (He is watching TV in the living room when she and Mr. Bascomb drive in and he barely makes it up to his room before the front door opens.)

When she calls him, he pretends not to hear, nor does he answer when she comes upstairs and knocks at the door of his room, which he has locked.

"Charles," she says in a low voice. "Won't you please come downstairs and meet Mr. Bascomb?"

When he greets the request with silence—he hopes she might think he is asleep—her voice changes to a low-pitched, angry hiss. She tells him that he is acting like a five-year-old child, and that if he doesn't get downstairs right this minute and be introduced to Mr. Bascomb—all he has to do, she insists, is say "hello" —she doesn't know what she will do.

This threat, which she has resorted to in the last year, fails to move him and she goes back downstairs to make some excuse or other to Mr. Bascomb, who shortly drives away.

It turns out that what his mother will "do" is give him the "silent treatment," which he can take pretty well. She does not speak to him at six o'clock when she fixes him some supper, nor does she address him at breakfast this morning. (There has been no "digesting" of the newspaper today.) Charles is beginning to get the uncomfortable feeling that he has acted like a fool as far as Mr. Bascomb is concerned.

From the parking area, Jeff gently tootles the horn of his car to indicate that if Charles doesn't hurry up, go in the building, see Miss Shrinking, and get it over with he is going to drive away and leave him.

Charles slouches in, gives his name to a woman in a peasant blouse who is pecking away at a typewriter behind a glass partition, and says he has come to see Miss Shrinking.

She appears almost at once and conducts him

to her office, which has so many plants and hanging baskets that he almost needs a machete to hack his way through.

Miss Shrinking is pleasant but businesslike. After letting it be known that she has talked to Daisy she says, "Well, Charles, what are your plans?"

Charles, who has no plans beyond not letting his baby be adopted, has difficulty swallowing. Finally he says that he is still thinking things over.

Miss Shrinking says that excuse does not wash. That unless Charles himself is prepared to set up housekeeping and care for the baby or find some other responsible adult to do so for him, it is a matter for the courts. Here she becomes almost severe. "Though some girls find the hassle of a court hearing so distasteful they wind up keeping the baby themselves, I do not think this will happen in Daisy's case."

"A court hearing?" says Charles, who has forgotten this is hanging over him.

Miss Shrinking says, "Oh, yes. As the baby's father, Charles, you have the right to be heard, but as I have been counseling you, you must not put *your* rights ahead of the baby's, who has a good home waiting for him as soon as you sign the release. The judge will decide where the best interests of the baby lie." She concludes, quite kindly, as he is leaving, "I am sure, Charles, you do not want to leave your baby suspended in limbo."

Charles promises to call her not later than Friday.

When he gets back to the car where Jeff is waiting, he asks him if he knows what limbo is. Jeff does
not, although he has heard of it. Charles seems so dis-
traught that he doesn't want to tell him he has this
idea that it isn't anything good.

12
FAMILY TIES

Charlotte (Charles is named for her) Penrose
lives in the same comfortable white-framed cottage—
over the years a new wing and a large screened porch
have been added—she moved into soon after marrying
Theodore Penrose more than forty years ago this coming December.

For thirty of those years—Pamela was ten when
her father died—she has been a widow, adapting to it
with an intelligence and lack of self-pity that everyone
admires.

Whenever she's had no "in-home" responsibility
—after Pam's husband left her and until Charles started
school the two lived with her—she has held down good
jobs. Last summer, when she decided to retire and enjoy

herself, she was working as a public relations counselor for a Cedar City bank.

Today, she is "enjoying" herself with the preliminary preparation for the luncheon she is giving the next day for her study club when the telephone rings.

"Oh, hello, Charles," she says. "What's new?"

"Oh, nothing much," says Charles. "I was just wondering how you were."

"Fine. Fine." She turns off the heat under the fresh mushrooms being sautéed in clear butter and says, "How are *you?*"

"I'm fine, too," says Charles. "I thought if you were going to be home I'd drive over and show you my new car."

She says "marvelous," that she is going to be there, and to come along right away.

Returning to the kitchen, she is more than a little puzzled. Although Charles loved her dearly up to the age of ten or eleven—and she still thinks he loves her, but in a different way—of recent years there has been a subtle change. Although always polite and dutiful—Pamela has seen to that—Charlotte Penrose would be considerably less sharp than she is if she did not know that Charles practically never calls unless he wants something. It amuses her.

Taking the puff pastry out of the refrigerator, she rolls it and gives it another turn. Perhaps, she thinks, she has been doing the child an injustice. Perhaps he really *does* want to show her his new car.

13
WHEELS

Charles, slouching low in the seat of the Olds, is on his way to his grandmother's house. Although the weather is chilly, the window is down. His elbow is draped over the window ledge and the radio is turned as high as it will go. He is driving carefully because people are watching him. He knows this because every time he stops for a red light and another car draws abreast of him he can feel the driver looking at him and can almost hear him commenting on the good condition of that '69 Olds 98 and the expertise with which it is being handled by that young kid.

Charles has had his car for only a little more than twenty-four hours. He still cannot believe that it is his. Bought and paid for. Mingled with pride of ownership is a feeling of satisfaction with the "rightness" of that ownership. It's as if he were intended to have it. How else is it possible to explain the weird set of circumstances that led to its acquisition? First of all, if he had not stayed all night with Jeff Kline on Saturday night he would not have been eating breakfast there Sunday morning when Jeff's father comes in and sits down at the kitchen table to talk to him and Jeff. Right?

Charles has gone over the scene in his mind a dozen times, but he still can't remember how or why—for they've been talking baseball—the subject of cars comes up. But it does. And he just happens to mention that as soon as school is out he's going to be in the market for a good used car. The remark, however, must have stuck in Mr. Kline's mind, for the next night, which is Monday, the telephone rings and his mother calls up and says it's for him.

He is afraid it might be Miss Shrinking or Lucy Twining, who, every time he turns around, is offering him a joint or a drive somewhere, which he always refuses. The phone call, however, turns out to be from Mr. Kline, who gets to the point right away. It seems that there's this security officer at the plant where he works—a fellow by the name of Dombach—who, when he comes to work that morning, asks him if he knows anybody who's in the market for a good used car. A '69 Olds 98. Before calling Charles, Mr. Kline himself looks at it and drives it around the yard at the plant. He thinks it's a good buy.

Four doors and air-conditioned, it's got 58,000 miles on it, but this fellow Dombach has been its only owner and, except for tires which have still got a little wear in them, it's in top condition. The only thing, Mr. Kline goes on to say, is that Dombach wants cash on the line because *he's* got a chance to buy an Olds '75

113

Cutlass, four-door, V-8, air conditioned, with PS, DB, and radial tires, that he's going to have to pay cash for.

Charles almost faints when Mr. Kline asks him, first, if he's interested, and second, does he have nine hundred and fifty dollars cash on the line.

Charles says he is, and he does. Mr. Kline then puts Jeff, who is almost as excited as Charles is, on the line and the two of them figure out that by skipping lunch the next day they'll have time to take a run out to the plant and take a quick look at the car.

It is the first time since learning he is a father that Charles has something else to think about, and that is all he does think about—to the considerable detriment of his schoolwork—until twelve fifteen Tuesday when he and Jeff pull up before the plant's locked gates. Dombach himself is waiting for them and tells the guard who's on duty to let them in.

Although Charles has been telling himself that the Olds can't be as good as Mr. Dombach or Mr. Kline says it is, it turns out to be even better. They inspect it first in the employee's parking lot and Charles's heart climbs into his throat. It is the original paint job—a bright dark blue. The chrome glistens. Mr. Dombach points out the dents, which aren't all that many, and a cigarette burn in the off-white vinyl upholstery in the front seat. He kicks the tires, which aren't as badly worn as Charles has anticipated, then he gets in the back seat while Charles, Jeff beside him, drives the car from one end of the plant to the other. It's a big plant and there's one stretch of pavement that parallels a railway siding, where Charles is invited to accelerate to fifty-five miles an hour as a test.

Mr. Dombach says he doesn't want to press Charles for an answer, but there's another person who is interested in it and he'd really like to know today.

Charles's voice breaks as he tells Mr. Dombach that he'll take it. He explains that he has to work that afternoon, after school, but the next day he'll get his money out of the bank—Mr. Kline has advised a cashier's check—deliver it to Mr. Dombach, and pick up his car.

It is all accomplished without a hitch—even Charles's mother does not demur when he tells her what he is going to do (another miracle)—and at four thirty Wednesday he hands Mr. Dombach a certified check for nine hundred and fifty dollars and Mr. Dombach hands over the title to the car, the driver's manual, and a set of keys in a nice leather case. Charles drives off. Even sitting down he is six feet tall.

Since then, he is in a state of euphoria because he knows he was *meant* to have this car. For one thing, it makes it a lot easier to go see his grandmother, with whom he has not been in touch for some little time.

In fact, since Mr. Kline called on Monday night, he has had only one bad moment. That comes when he buys the cashier's check to give to Mr. Dombach and reflects briefly that if he had not given Daisy the money for the abortion he'd have one hundred and fifty dollars instead of practically zilch in his account.

14
GRANDMA'S HOUSE

Charlotte Penrose, whose friends call her "Char," is looking out the living room window when Charles drives into her driveway. She puts a sweater around her shoulders and goes out to meet him and inspect the car.

Charles finds her reaction gratifying. His grandmother likes cars, understands them. (At present, she is driving—at least, as far as he knows, not having seen her for several months—a dark green '74 Monte Carlo Landau 350 V-8, with everything, including an AM-FM 8-track with CB in the dash, air-conditioning, and cruise control).

She wants to know who owned the Olds before he did, how much it cost, everything about it. He tells her. She continues to be impressed and allows him to drive her around the block, then over to the shopping center, where she buys some long johns at Mister Donut, and back again. She then asks him if he has time to come in. Actually, his grandmother is pretty smart.

116

Even with the long johns as a lure, Charlotte Penrose is a bit surprised that he comes in. She is, in fact, already feeling a little guilty that she allowed any negative thoughts about Charles's reason for visiting her to enter her mind.

When she goes out to the kitchen, he follows her. "I bet it gets pretty lonesome around here sometimes," he says. "I mean, you living here all alone, and everything." He lounges up against the refrigerator and she has to ask him to move so she can get the milk out, but he does not take offense.

Charlotte Penrose says that, well, maybe, sometimes she gets lonesome, but after all these years she is pretty well used to living by herself.

Charles gently corrects what he believes to be a misunderstanding of his question. "Of course, you're *used* to it," he says, "but, I mean, it would depend, wouldn't it, on who it was? I mean, like you wouldn't want just anybody living with you. Somebody who talked all the time, or who wanted the TV on when you wanted to read. That would be gross. But, maybe, somebody young?"

For an alarmed moment Charles's grandmother wonders if her daughter Pamela and Charles are considering moving in with her, but rejects the idea as preposterous. She laughs. Even before Pam came into a rather decent inheritance from her father's brother, she had managed well by herself from the time Charles started kindergarten.

117

His grandmother's laugh encourages Charles to continue. "By young," he says, "I mean *really* young. Like a baby."

Charlotte Penrose's laugh ricochets around the pretty blue and white kitchen. "What in the world would I do with a *baby?*" Her tight, white curls rise like antennae.

For a moment, Charles is too taken aback to reply. Finally, he stutters out a response. "To . . . to keep you from getting lonesome . . . to kind of give you something to do . . ."

Charlotte Penrose is no longer laughing. She says, "Perhaps, Charles, you'd better tell me just what it is you are talking about." She goes on to say that, among other things, she'd like to know if there's a particular baby he has in mind.

Charles takes a long time to swallow a bit of long john, then says, well, yes, there is. That he's got this friend who's got a baby he would kind of like to keep in touch with, but that, since he doesn't want to get married right now, he has this problem. . . . His voice trails off because his grandmother is looking at him in a way he does not like at all. A long minute passes, however, before she asks him if, by chance, this baby he's talking about belongs to that nice boy Jeff Something-or-other whom she's met a couple of times.

Charles does not blink an eye when he says it does.

15
LIMBO

That night Charles sleeps poorly.

He keeps thinking about how he messed up the opportunity to get a home for his baby at his grandmother's house, though he still doesn't know why she doesn't want to do it. He's sorry that he got Jeff Kline mixed up in it. He thinks about Daisy, who loves fresh air and water, cooped up with her Aunt Nelda in a couple of rooms in the brown house on Holbrook Avenue, and he thinks about his mother, who's been out with Mr. Bascomb for three nights in a row.

In other ways, too, his situation is very tight. Although his mother is talking to him, she's pretty distant. In fact, she's really laid down a kind of ultimatum. She says that when he's ready to act in a civilized manner and meet Mr. Bascomb he is to let her know. She has met Mr. Bascomb's son Daryl, who goes to the State University, and he is very nice. Charles thinks, but does not say, Daisy's favorite word. He remembers that he has promised to go see Miss Shrinking on Friday and that he still has nothing to tell her.

But most of all, he thinks about his baby. He tries to remember exactly how he looks but the vision of his face, the little smile, and the small waving fists is fading like a color snapshot that's exposed to sunlight. He is stricken by a terrible thought. Perhaps the reason he cannot "see" his baby is because he is suspended in limbo.

He still does not know what limbo is.

It is after one o'clock when he finally turns on the lamp by his bed and goes downstairs. Only a small night-light is burning in the living room and he must turn on a table lamp in order to read the small type in the big dictionary which he takes from the bookcase.

He runs a forefinger down a page of *l*s: limb, limbate, limber . . . limberham . . . limbic lobe, limbiferous . . . At last, he comes to "limbo." His throat contracts as he reads: "The abode of souls barred from heaven through no fault of their own: of just men who died before the coming of Christ, or of unbaptized infants (limbo infantum, so-called, because it was believed by theologians to lie on the confines of hell)."

Charles turns out the light and goes back to bed, but until his mother comes home and he finally drops off to sleep, he can see his baby suspended (in a kind of crude macramé holder) over a chasm in the earth in which a few flames lick fitfully around the bones of just men—and infants, barred from heaven through no fault of their own.

16
THE DREAM

Soon after falling asleep, Charles has a dream.

In the dream, he is sitting on a boulder over-hanging a mountain lake. He is holding a fly rod and from time to time he casts it out over the water, where it holds its shape for a moment in a perfect arc, then, with the lure winking and blinking like a blue and scarlet eye, it cuts through the surface of the lake.

A moment later, he feels a tug on the line, then with consummate skill he winds the reel, gives play to the line, reels in again; then a rainbow trout lies gasping beside him on the rock. He measures it mentally (it is a half-inch too small), then throws it back into the water.

It is then he sees the canoe coming slowly toward him from the far side of the lake. A man—Charles can see that he is a tall man even though he is sitting down —is at the oars. The oars split the water clearly, silently, until the canoe reaches the shore a hundred or so yards away, where the man expertly beaches it and, with the walk of a woodsman, an outdoorsman, comes toward him.

He is dressed in deerskin. He is young, lithe, and there is a cleft in his chin. Yet there is something strange about him, too. Charles can see through him, as one sees through gauze, to the other side of the lake where stunted trees huddle near the shore.

The man speaks, but Charles has difficulty hearing him. They try to embrace but they cannot hold each other closely. Tears come to the man's eyes as he says he has come back from the other side for the purpose of confessing his mistake in going away and leaving him, and that when he wanted to come back it was too late.

Already the sun is going down. Mist rises over the lake and a sleepy bird whistles a soft "too late, too late, too late" from the branches of a pine tree. As the man gets into the canoe and pushes off from the shore, his last words are, "Whatever you do, my boy, keep your son." A second later, man and canoe are lost in the mist.

The dream is so real it awakens him. Although he does not get to sleep again, the time is not wasted. By morning he has figured out a way to keep his baby.

BOOK THREE

The King shuddered. He went up to the
room over the gate and weeping said, "My
son, Absolom, would God I had died for
thee! O! Absolom, my son, my son!"
—II Samuel 18:33

1
ACCOMMODATION

At breakfast that morning, Charles tells his mother that he would like very much to meet Mr. Bascomb. He says he is sorry he has acted so badly. He'd like to meet Mr. Bascomb's son Daryl, too, and get acquainted.

Pamela Elderbury is overjoyed. Pitifully so. She hugs him. Tears come to her eyes and she brushes them away saying she is silly. But they—she and Mr. Bascomb—as soon as they can, will work out something nice so they can all spend an evening together, and she goes to work twittering childishly.

As soon as his mother is out of the house, Charles calls Miss Shrinking and says he will stop in to see her on Friday as she asked him to, that he now has a plan to keep his baby but will need a few more days to work out the details.

Clearly, Miss Shrinking does not believe he has a plan but she says, yes, he can have until the first of the week. She adds that she has talked to Daisy, who is upset by the delay and wants to put the matter of the baby's adoption into the hands of the court.

"The court?" says Charles hollowly.

"Why, yes," says Miss Shrinking. "That's the next step."

Charles tells her stiffly that he doesn't think the next step will be necessary and that if he doesn't hang up he will be late for school.

2
FRIENDSHIP

That afternoon, Charles meets Jeff Kline in the parking lot after school. He's due at work shortly, so he gets right to the point. He tells Jeff he's worked out a plan to keep the baby, but that he's going to need some help.

When Jeff says he'll do anything he can, Charles explains that every time he sees Miss Shrinking at the Allied Social Services Agency she is carrying this folder with DALLINGER-ELDERBURY written on the tab, and that he's got another appointment to see her the next day, which is Friday. While he's there, he wants Jeff to get Miss Shrinking out of her office just long enough for him to look in the folder—he doesn't care how Jeff does it—and find out the name of the foster family keeping his baby. He draws a little floor plan of the first floor that shows where the receptionist sits and where Miss Shrinking holds out. Although there are other offices on the first floor, they are at the end of a long hall, and Charles thinks that in a crisis the receptionist would run for Miss Shrinking.

Jeff says this will take some thinking, but obviously the idea appeals to him. He promises he will come up with something and they let it go at that.

Charles leaves Jeff and goes to Farley's, where he is put to work sacking for Macho Muriel. He has not been on the job for thirty minutes when, aiming for the sack with FARLEY'S—WE SELL FOR LESS BECAUSE IT SAVES YOU MONEY on the side, he drops a large-size bottle of Diablo spaghetti sauce on the floor. Not daring to move, he freezes in position. But instead of treating him to the vituperation he expects, Macho Muriel is beating herself on the forehead with a fist as big as a grapefruit, saying in a loud voice, "Christ Almighty! How clumsy can a person get?" She yells for the kitty litter, which Mr. Farley himself brings her, saying soothingly as he does so that "Accidents will happen."

It is not until the mess is cleaned up that Macho says, "Listen, kid. I'm worried about you. You're not yourself lately. You know? It's nothing to be ashamed of. I mean, if you've got the clap or something worse you'd better see a doctor. I've got a friend who's a sort of specialist in that kind of thing." And she

127

gives him a dig in the ribs with her elbow that almost doubles him up.

3
THE PERFORMANCE

Jeff is sitting hunched up in the seat of his car when Charles drives into the parking lot of the Allied Social Services Agency the next afternoon.

Charles, who has been as jumpy as a cat on a hot tin roof ever since he dropped the spaghetti sauce, gives no sign of greeting but goes into the office, where he gives his name to the woman in the peasant blouse sitting behind the glass window with the hole in it. He says he has an appointment with Miss Shrinking.

As he sits waiting, he grows more and more nervous. His mouth is dry and his palms are wet. If he is unable to find out the name of the foster family who is keeping the baby, the whole plan goes up in smoke. He is reminded of the daytime TV serial he watched (for lack of anything better to do) last winter, when he was home from school for a week with a strained ligament in his ankle. Will Jeff be able to get Miss Shrinking out of the office so he can look in the folder? How will Jeff do it? (Several possibilities occur to him, any one of which could result in the police being called and the whole thing ruined.) Charles wishes he had told Jeff, whose brain is notoriously fertile, to use *caution*.

Charles is anticipating the worst when Miss Shrinking, carrying the DALLINGER-ELDERBURY folder between thumb and pinkie, appears and takes him back to her office.

"Well, Charles," says Miss Shrinking, "naturally I'm glad to see you but as you will be coming in on Monday with your plan to keep the baby"—her voice, though pleasant, is plenty sarcastic—"I should think your time might be better spent working on it."

Charles replies that, in a way, he *is* working on it and that he is coming in today only because she had requested it.

The two look at each other. Charles hopes that his nervousness does not show, for Miss Shrinking has laid the DALLINGER-ELDERBURY folder on the desk and it is not more than a foot away from his right hand, which lies twitching in his lap.

Miss Shrinking breaks the silence. "Perhaps, Charles," she says—she is amiable again—"you'd like to tell me a little something about the plan you are working on."

Charles, who has been expecting this question, is prepared to say he would prefer not to talk about the plan until it is perfected. However, no reply is necessary, for the door to the office is thrown open and the woman who sits behind the glass partition with the hole in it comes bursting in.

"Vida!" she screams. "Vi! Come quickly. A boy ... a big boy ... he's having a ... an ... he's down on the floor ... *writhing* ..."

Miss Shrinking rises from her desk. "Calm yourself, Ruby," she says, but she's not all that calm herself, and in a second the two of them are hightailing it out the door and Charles is alone with the folder. Divine Providence is at work. The Lord is hearing his prayer. For the first sheet of paper, of the many in the folder, bears the name of the woman who is caring for the baby. *"Mrs. Cora Wanamaker of 1414 Willow Street,"* he reads. In an instant, it is engraved on his mind forever.

He is looking out the window into an alley when Miss Shrinking returns to the office a minute or two later. "How peculiar," she says. "How *very* peculiar ..."

Although Charles has the distinct impression that Miss Shrinking is not talking to him, he turns and says, "Pardon me?"

Miss Shrinking goes on, as if talking to herself. "The young man demanding to see me *must* have had an epileptic fit ... but that it should have been of such short duration. And how very peculiar that when I appeared there was no one there at all ..."

Charles says politely that he thinks he had better be going. And he does.

130

4
COMMON BOND

Charles goes directly from Miss Shrinking's office to Farley's, where he starts looking for Hubert Turnquist. He finds him taking a break in the employees' "day room."

This day room is right next to the men's and women's rest rooms and here it is possible for employees of either sex to sit down—lie down, if they wish, for Mr. Farley, despite his faults, is a thoughtful as well as an equal rights employer—smoke a cigarette, drink a cup of coffee or a soft drink, and eat a sandwich.

Hubert Turnquist offers Charles a Hostess cupcake from the open package beside him and goes on looking at a big stack of color snapshots. Charles can see at a glance that they are of a baby. He has not hoped for such luck. This is why he has come looking for Hubert: to talk about babies. He looks over Hubert's shoulder. "Oh, your baby!" he says enthusiastically. "May I see the pictures?"

Gratified, Hubert starts handing the pictures to

131

Charles, explaining each one as he does. Charles looks at Baby Orville asleep and Baby Orville awake. He sees him being held, respectively, by Mommy, Daddy, Grandma Fedderson, and Grandpa Turnquist. He is allowed an intimate view of Baby Orville being bathed, drinking from his bottle, and being burped. All this and more. Much, much more.

Looking at them with feigned interest, Charles from time to time makes flattering comments like, "Good-looking baby," or "Husky little fellow," though he does not really think so.

Not until Hubert regretfully puts the snapshots back in the yellow envelope does Charles, in the most casual of voices, get down to business. "A person has got to have pretty much stuff, I bet, to take care of a baby."

Hubert, afraid that the statement implies some criticism of Baby Orville, is cautious in his reply. "Pretty much," he says, "but not too much."

"Well, I mean, like what?"

"Well," says Hubert, "he's got to have something to sleep in. He'll have to have a crib later on, but at first almost anything will do. A basket . . . a cradle . . . you know . . ."

Charles, who has been worrying about this, thinks a good sturdy box from produce (lined with something soft) might do. Cheered, he says, "Go on."

Hubert, however, still hesitates long enough that Charles finds it necessary to state his position. "I want to know," he says, "because of this friend who's having a baby before too long. I mean, his wife's having it. Maybe tomorrow."

With this information, Hubert warms to the subject and asks if the wife of Charles's friend is planning to nurse her baby. Assured that she is not—and this is one thing Charles *is* sure of—Hubert says that, first off, they'll have to have nursing bottles, nipples, and a bottle brush. "But," he adds, "I think they can get along without a sterilizer."

This, thinks Charles, is rather blunt talk. He doesn't think anyone would want to get sterilized after just one baby, but he is afraid to inquire any further. He continues to write down everything except "sterilizer" on a paper napkin he has picked up from the floor.

"They'd better lay in a pretty good supply of Kwiksies," says Hubert.

"Kwiksies?" asks Charles. "What are Kwiksies?"

"Diapers, man," says Hubert, displaying a side of his character that Charles has never seen before. "They're the paper kind you throw away, and, man! Are they ever going to need those!"

"I guess maybe that's all?" inquires Charles hopefully.

Hubert's laugh is slightly maniacal. "Not by a long shot. They'll need some of those little toothpicks with cotton on the end, some wrapping blankets, and some . . ."

Charles interrupts to ask the nature of the toothpicks with the cotton but skips the business of the wrapping blankets, which he has interpreted as "rapping" blankets. (He wonders how anyone can rap with a baby!)

Hubert admits he doesn't know what the tooth-picks are for, but he says that Audrey has a whole lot of them. He then takes out the envelope full of snapshots and asks if Charles would like to look at them again.

Charles says he would like to, but the father of the soon-to-be-born baby is in the hospital with a broken leg and he has promised to pick up the "neces-sities" for him.

Hubert says, "Wow, that *is* tough," and reminds Charles that he can buy most of the things his friend needs right here at Farley's at a discount.

Charles, who is not unmindful of this factor, thanks Hubert for his help and goes out to do his shopping.

It takes him almost an hour. When he leaves the supermarket, he has bought two nursing bottles—though one, to him, seems plenty, a baby being only able to drink out of one bottle at a time—a bottle brush, three wrapping blankets (the printing on the package cleared up his confusion about "rapping"), two nipples (nasty-looking rubber things which do not look like anything that grows on Daisy), a pacifier (nasty-looking, also, though he has seen lots of babies in the store with these plugs in their mouths), a package of Q-tips (the toothpicks with the cotton on the end, whose use is still obscure), a bottle brush, baby powder, baby soap, baby oil, and a twelve-pack of Kwiksies.

This leaves him with one dollar and seventeen

134

cents in his pocket and four dollars and eighty-three
cents in his savings account at the Cedar City National
Bank, the latter amount being what was left after he
bought his Olds 98. It will be a long time before he can
buy his water bed and move to the basement, which will
be necessary if Mr. Bascomb should move in with
them, but he tries not to think about that unhappy day.

He then goes to a pay phone up near the
Courtesy Counter and calls Jeff to tell him what a great
job he did getting Miss Shrinking out of her office,
and that he accomplished *his* mission.

Jeff modestly says it was nothing. He just staged
a little epileptic fit. He adds, however, that to make it
more realistic he had taken along a plastic bottle filled
with soapy water and that while Miss Peasant Blouse
was fetching Miss Shrinking he had, before departing,
squirted a pile of froth on the floor.

Next, Charles gives his friend a new project.
It is, he says, to think of the best way for him, Charles,
to get inside the house at 1414 Willow Street without
actually breaking and entering, this event to take place
the next day. (He does not tell Jeff *why* he wants in,
because he is sure he already knows.) Jeff says to call
him at ten o'clock that night and that by then he will
have thought of something.

Well pleased with the way everything is working out, Charles goes to produce, where he finds a
sturdy cardboard carton with handholds cut in either
end, which will serve very nicely as a temporary bed
for his baby. He then goes home to make ready.

135

5
THE BIG LIE

Charles is afraid his mother will be home before he is, but he gets there in plenty of time to smuggle in his purchases and fix up the cardboard carton with some kind of a knitted shawl thing he finds in one of his mother's dresser drawers. He puts the whole works in his closet.

When his mother arrives, she is laden down with several large sacks of groceries. They will not be eating out of the Crock Pot *tonight,* she says. She has bought steak, fresh mushrooms, french-fried potatoes to finish in the oven, stuff for salad, and a frozen cherry pie. She is, in fact, so giddy all through dinner that he is not surprised when, afterward, she asks him to come into the living room for a "little talk."

Usually the expression "little talk" is a sign that his mother is about to bring up something that is distasteful to him, but tonight he greets the words almost with joy. He feels benevolent toward his mother. Protective. (He is now considerably taller than she is and every day he is growing taller.) As she asks him to sit down, he thinks he knows what she wants to talk to him about.

He feels sure of it when she gives him a look that is almost frightened. "I hope, Charles," she says, "that this isn't too much of a shock. As you know I've been wanting you to meet Mr. Bascomb ever since he started asking me out . . ."

"I guess I've acted pretty childish," Charles says in his deepest voice.

"I hope you won't be too surprised . . . I mean, I hope you won't mind if we marry rather soon . . . but not, of course, unless you agree . . . he's a fine man . . . lonely . . . I . . ."

His mother is getting so bogged down in her own rhetoric that Charles feels sorry for her. He says he does not mind if she marries Mr. Bascomb. He wants to add "the sooner the better" but he does not want to go overboard. His mother hugs him.

"Can you imagine," she asks, "your mother not working after all these years? No more dinners out of the Crock Pot? Staying home with nothing to *do* all day?"

All of this is exactly what Charles *has* been imagining. If his mother marries Mr. Bascomb and quits her job she will be home all day to take care of the baby. And what could be nicer than that?

6
SNATCH

On Saturdays Charles works the eight A.M. to noon shift at Farley's. That he will have the afternoon free, is, Charles thinks, another indication of the rightness of his plan.

He eats a good breakfast which his mother, who does not ordinarily get up on Saturday mornings, fixes him. She is going, she says, "antiquing," and will not be home until later that afternoon but she will be home that night since Mr. Bascomb is going to a Phi Gamma Delta alumni dinner.

At work, Charles is too busy to worry about the next and most dangerous part of the plan. This is the business of getting himself *in* and the baby *out* of Mrs. Cora Wanamaker's house. To accomplish this, he is depending on a clipboard with several sheets of paper attached to it. With this in hand, he will say he is from the City Assessor's office. (All this is Jeff's idea—transmitted the night before—and Charles thinks it is a good one.) Once he is invited into Mrs. Wanamaker's house, he is sure he will soon be able to establish the whereabouts of the baby. Before leaving and after looking around in all the rooms and asking questions about what he hopes are her "assessable possessions," he will be seized with a coughing spell and ask politely for a drink of water. While Mrs. Wanamaker is getting it, he will simply pick up the baby and leave. If this ruse fails, Jeff has provided several alternate plans, but Charles does not even want to think about these as they are pretty far out.

Charles does not consider what he is about to do kidnapping. The baby, he reasons, is his. (Daisy does not want it.) His mother will only have to *see* the baby to be won over completely. How could she not? Is not this baby flesh of his mother's flesh and blood of his mother's blood? (He does not know from where these words suddenly appear in his mind, but they seem singularly appropriate.) That she—*they*, really, because he plans to contribute—will have to hire a sitter to care for the baby until she marries Mr. Bascomb (which should be soon) is not too big a price to pay to have the baby raised an Elderbury.

7

CHANGES MADE

Charles does not know where Willow Street is and stops at a gas station to find out. The attendant does not know where it is either, but obligingly gets out a map of the city and looks it up.

It is, Charles finds, on the city's near northeast side. He takes the freeway to the East Twelfth Street exit, then works his way over to East Fourteenth Street and then goes north until it is intersected by Willow Street, which proves to be a neighborhood of modest older houses.

Charles proceeds slowly. Even before he spots the house number, 1414, he sees the big, old-fashioned baby buggy on the porch of a white, one-story frame house which sits on a corner lot. His heart starts knocking on his ribs as if asking to come out.

He turns the corner. A middle-aged woman with her hair in curlers and wearing a baggy sweater is in the backyard hanging up long flapping white rectangles on a clothesline stretched between the garage and a tree. So far she has hung up at least a dozen, but the clothes basket at her feet still seems to be heaped with them.

Charles speeds up, circles the block, and stops in front of the house, leaving the motor running and the clipboard, which he will not need now, in the car. He goes up the sidewalk and onto the porch. He looks around him. Not a car, not a person is in sight. He bends over the buggy and peers in. The baby, wearing a cap with bunny ears, is asleep. He is lying on his stomach, his face turned to one side and pressed into a pillow. The rest of him is tucked in tightly under a fuzzy blue blanket. Charles loosens the blanket but he does not know how to pick a baby up. He forces himself, somehow, to get the baby out of the buggy. The baby is not as heavy as he had thought it would be. It does not seem to have any bones. Its head is falling this way and that. He tries holding it for a minute along one arm the way the nurse in the hospital did, but almost drops it. He then puts the baby upon his shoulder, manages to drape the blanket around it, and then walks down the sidewalk, opens the car door, and puts the baby in the box which he has placed on the floor next to the driver's seat.

As Charles pulls away from the curb the baby, who by some miracle has so far remained asleep, screws up his face and starts to make faint mewing sounds. By the time he reaches the freeway, the baby is really crying. At work, Charles has heard lots of children crying, but he has no idea that a *little* baby can cry so loudly. He remembers that the newborn babies at the hospital were crying behind *glass*.

The crying is making him nervous. Out of the corner of his eye he can see the baby waving his fists around. They look like small red dough balls stuck on the end of two pink sticks. He has also kicked both feet out from the blue blanket. Although he has seen the baby's feet before, he has not seen his legs. They are bent like the hind legs of a frog, and it comes to him that perhaps his baby is deformed. With a cramp in his gut, he leaves the freeway an exit too soon and brings the car to a stop on a side street.

Charles is horrified. The nightgown thing the baby is wearing has come open down the front and his undershirt is hiked up. Where his belly button ought to be there is a protuberance that looks like an over-sized pencil eraser; also some dried blood. He covers it up with the flaps of the nightgown thing and then puts the blue blanket over that.

He does not go back on the freeway but takes the longer route home. By the time he gets there, his hands are perspiring so he can hardly hold the steering wheel. He gets the baby, who is still yelling his head off, into the house and up to his room, where he starts rummaging for and finally finds the pacifier among the supplies he bought the day before. It is encased in hard plastic and he has to make a trip to the kitchen to get a paring knife to extract it.

The baby seems a little quieter by the time he gets back upstairs but as soon as he thrusts the pacifier into the baby's mouth, which is dark red like a fish's gullet, it promptly falls out. His eyes, which had seemed so deep and dark and full of ancient wisdom, are mere slits in a face that is no longer red but becoming purple. In fact, this baby is like all the other crying inferior babies he had seen in the hospital. Only more so.

Charles wishes his mother would come and take over. On the other hand, he's afraid that if the baby doesn't stop crying she will get a bad impression.

In desperation, he scoops the baby out of the produce box and holds it up to his shoulder, a position that the baby had seemed to like earlier. Now, however, it holds no more magic than the pacifier. The baby also seems disagreeably moist. A brown stain is seeping out of the side of its diaper and comes off on his hand. He looks at it, averts his face. "Oh, no," he says to himself. "Oh, no." But there is no doubt that it is. Although it does help explain why the baby is crying, he wishes it hadn't happened right now. He does not know whether he will be able to get the soiled diaper off and a clean one on, but he intends to try. He remembers how Jeff put a sort of knee-chest lock on his little brother Joey, but his baby is too little for that.

He gets a Kwiksie out of the twelve-pack he bought. He retches as he removes the soiled diaper—it is made of cloth like the ones hanging on the line at 1414 Willow Street—and tries to wash the baby fore and aft with a wet washcloth he has fetched from the bathroom. After that, it takes him some little time and three Kwiksies—to him, they seem most inappropriately named—before he gets the job done. Even then it is half off and half on.

The whole operation has so infuriated the baby that he has started crying harder than ever.

Charles lifts his eyes to the ceiling, beyond which lies heaven, and says, "Oh! God!" Whereupon, a strange thing happens. Charles is quite sure he hears a deep voice say, "Yes?" in an inquiring tone.

"What'll I do?" whimpers Charles. "Oh, God! What'll I do?"

(Later, when Charles tells Jeff about the conversation, Jeff believes him when he says God answered his question. "Why not?" says Jeff. "Lots of times God tells people what to do, but they've got to listen.")

In any event, it is answer enough for Charles. Less than five minutes later, he has the baby back in the produce box, covers him with the blue blanket, and puts him back in the car. He takes the freeway, exiting as before on Twelfth Street. Somewhere along the route —he does not know exactly where—he becomes aware of the fact that the baby is no longer crying.

8
UP THE WALL

As he drives along, Charles, so far, has given no thought as to how he is going to return the baby. It is enough to know that he is doing the right thing. He knows deep in his heart that Daisy, living with Aunt Nelda in one or two rooms, cannot raise this baby as he should be raised. As for his mother, who will soon be starting a new life with Mr. Bascomb, she should not *have* to. And equally important, he knows he cannot. Repeat, he says to himself, *cannot*. In the short period of time that he has had the baby, the kid has driven him almost up the wall.

9
JETTISONED

The first thing that Charles sees when he turns the corner onto Willow Street is a patrol car sitting in the driveway of 1414. Now that he sees it there, he realizes that he should have known that as soon as Mrs. Wanamaker missed the baby she would call the police, and that he will probably have more trouble returning the baby than he did in taking him.

He hurriedly drives around the corner and on around the block, his heart knocking as if it needs new spark plugs. There are only three things to encourage him: One, the baby is still asleep; two, the patrol car seems to be exciting no curiosity at all. (Had a patrol car driven into *his* driveway on Meadowlark Lane, every kid in the neighborhood and half the adults would have been standing around in a circle waiting to see what would happen next.) And three, he determines that there is no cop in the patrol car. This means that he—or they, if there are two of them—is in Mrs. Wanamaker's house.

The baby is still sleeping when Charles takes

the produce box out of the Olds and puts it in the front seat of the patrol car. On his way home, before reaching the freeway, he sees two more patrol cars speeding in the direction of 1414 Willow Street.

10
AFTERMATH

Charles's mother is in the kitchen when he comes into the house.

She says, "Charles, is that you?"

He says it is. As he starts upstairs, she calls after him and asks if anything is wrong—it is his usual custom upon arriving home to go immediately to the kitchen to get a little something to eat—and he replies that there isn't. He just doesn't feel well.

She is out of the kitchen in a flash and follows him up to his room, where she stands outside his closed door. "What is it?" she asks. "Your stomach?"

She could not sound more worried, Charles thinks, if he had just announced that he was covered with red spots and was burning up with fever.

"Your . . . your *head?*"

"No, No, NO!" he replies, then adds in a calmer

tone that he just does not feel well, that's all, and all he wants is to be left alone.

"Very well, then," says his mother. "*I'll* leave you alone."

Unfortunately, she doesn't. He can feel her presence outside his closed door but he hardens his heart to her. She will marry Mr. Bascomb and shut him out of her life. He will have no one. Not even his baby.

11
A WISE FATHER

The next morning Charles's mother brings him his breakfast in bed and the Sunday paper. He says he is feeling better and the news greatly cheers her. Actually, he *is* feeling better. Although he has never had a really serious illness, he knows (or thinks he knows) how a critically ill patient must feel when he awakens one morning and he is no longer burning with fever, hallucinating, or simply not caring whether he lives or dies. (He feels like living.)

Charles finishes his breakfast and turns to the Sunday paper. It is in seven sections: general news, home and family, the arts, opinion, farming, sports, and want ads. He reads the sports section first, almost in its entirety. The home and family pages are next to catch his eye because on the front page there is a picture of Lucy Twining, along with a couple of other girls he knows who go to CCHS, wearing a striped uniform and delivering a potted plant to an elderly lady in a hospital bed. He is surprised to learn from the story that Lucy—he is not surprised about the other two girls—works two afternoons a week after school as a volunteer at the Cedar City Medical Center. Charles thinks that perhaps she isn't as empty-headed and dangerous as she lets on to be.

He discards the farm and opinion pages and turns to the general news. It is as bad as ever. A bomb goes off in Northern Ireland killing five people. In the Midwest, air pollutants reach a dangerous high. A new sex scandal hits Washington; Russia blasts U.S. foreign policy. A teenager from a suburban high school is critically injured (almost, but not quite, confirming Pamela Elderbury's prophecy) when he slams into the barricade erected by order of the City Council in Merrill Park.

Charles reads only the headlines and the first few paragraphs of all these stories—except for the one about the teenager injured at the barricade, of which he reads every word—which, because of their newsworthiness, have been situated in the upper half of the paper above the "fold."

He turns the paper, scans the stories below. There, he reads:

149

Sleeping Infant Stolen From
Front Porch of Foster Home

"Wow!" thinks Charles. "What a coincidence!"

He reads two paragraphs of the story before it hits him. They are talking about *him*. Even then, he cannot believe his eyes and goes back and, starting at the beginning, reads the story through to the end.

"A two-week-old baby who was kidnapped early yesterday afternoon while sleeping in his buggy on the front porch of Mrs. Cora Wanamaker, 1414 Willow Street, was returned unharmed to the same address less than an hour after his disappearance was reported to police.

"Mrs. Wanamaker, a court-approved foster mother in whose home the infant is being cared for until his adoption is finalized later this week, called police as soon as she found the baby missing. She had been hanging up diapers in the backyard, she said, and did not miss the baby until she came inside sometime later.

"Sergeant Lester Lightfoot, who was the first officer dispatched by police to the Willow Street address when the alarm came in, says that, when he came out of the house after interviewing Mrs. Wanamaker at some length, he found the infant in the front seat of his patrol car. Said Sergeant Lightfoot, 'You could have knocked me over with a feather.'

"Apparently, there were no witnesses either when the baby was stolen or returned.

"Miss Vida Shrinking, 24, a social worker for the agency handling the adoption, says that she believes a sixteen-year-old boy who is a client in another adoption case her agency is handling may have taken the baby. 'He possibly believed the baby to be his own,' says Miss Shrinking. 'If so, he is mistaken. A change in foster homes for the two infants, who are almost the same age, was made by the agency at the last minute. I think it is this circumstance which caused the confusion. The teenager's child, who will be adopted as soon as a dispute between him and the baby's sixteen-year-old mother is settled, is being cared for elsewhere.' "

Charles lies back in bed, weak with relief that everything has turned out so well. And perhaps the best news of all is that that screaming, ill-tempered, inferior baby so briefly in his possession was not his.

12
SOME GRANDMOTHER

Charles's mother makes no mention of the story in the Sunday paper. She is blinded by love. Also, Mr. Bascomb has returned from a visit to his son and she holds a long telephone conversation with him (Mr. Bascomb) and goes out with him later that evening.

While she's gone, Charles's grandmother calls. "I gather your mother's out?" she says.

Charles says she is.

"In that case," replies his grandmother, "we can talk freely. Which is to say that I read about your *friend* in the paper this morning."

Charles makes a choking sound.

"I hope your friend is not going to do anything *else* foolish," she says. "I'd think he'd let that baby be legally adopted by someone who really wants a baby."

"I'm going to," says Charles. "I mean, he—my friend—is going to, right after school tomorrow."

"I'm glad to hear that," says his grandmother, "and in that case, I think it would be best just to let the matter drop."

Charles thinks, Some grandmother! and replaces the receiver in the cradle.

13
FAREWELL, MISS SHRINKING

The signing of the adoption release papers the next day goes better than Charles expects. This is because Miss Shrinking does not mention the story that was in the Sunday paper. When he appears in her office, she smiles at him knowingly and says, "All's well that ends well," then she tells him she thinks he is making a wise decision. She adds that if he ever feels like coming in to talk to her about anything—about anything at all—he should please feel free to do so.

They shake hands, and that's it.

14
CHECK-OUT

Charles lets a couple of days go by before going to see Daisy. He does not expect her to jump into his arms, but he thinks that now he has signed the adoption release papers they can at least be friends. After all, summer is coming and, with Daisy living with her Aunt Nelda and with him having the Olds, getting back and forth to Lake Larkspur will be no trouble for either of them.

Up to the time he parks the car in front of the big brown house on the corner of Parkway and Holbrook, he still does not know how he is going to broach the subject of them getting together again. But as it turns out, there is no need.

His knock is answered by a woman with a face like a meat cleaver who tells him that whoever has lived there doesn't live there anymore and shuts the door in his face.

He next drives over to Daisy's old neighborhood. Because he's afraid of Daisy's father, he parks the car a quarter of a block away from the house and waits for Indigo to come along carrying her paper route. Pretty soon she does so, but this time Indigo is not friendly. "I'm not supposed to talk to you," she says, "ever again," and then speeds away on her bike as if she were being pursued by a mad rapist.

Because Charles is unable to find Daisy, he thinks about her a lot. It occurs to him that she has more sense than he has. He dreams about the two of them being together on the raft. He fantasizes that someday their paths will cross again and perhaps they might even marry. He experiences a twinge of guilt for putting Daisy out of his mind as soon as he sent her away to have an abortion. He knows it was wrong of him to hassle her about signing the adoption papers. And it was pretty cheap of him even to have wondered what happened to his one hundred and fifty dollars. If he could give her the money to have an abortion, why should he complain if she spent it to have a baby?

So he keeps on giving himself a hard time until Lucy Twining calls and asks him over to her house one night. A lot of other kids are there and he has a better time than he expects. Before long he and Lucy start going around together and soon after that Daisy's image begins rather rapidly to fade.

With the baby, however, it is a different matter. Even after his mother marries Mr. Bascomb (who turns out to be a shade better than he expects, which is no particular endorsement because he hasn't expected very much), he thinks about his son.

155

And as long as he works at Farley's, which is up to the time he starts college, he pays particular attention to all the babies who pass through the check-out counter with their mothers, hoping to see one with a cleft in his chin.